Discovering Pig Magic

DISCOVERING PIG MAGIC

Julie Crabtree

MILKWEED
EDITIONS

© 2008, Text by Julie Crabtree
All rights reserved. Except for brief quotations in critical articles or reviews, no part of this book may be reproduced in any manner without prior written permission from the publisher: Milkweed Editions, 1011 Washington Avenue South, Suite 300, Minneapolis, Minnesota 55415.
(800) 520-6455
www.milkweed.org

Published 2008 by Milkweed Editions
Printed in Canada
Cover design by Kristine Mudd
Cover photo by Lottie Davies / Digital Vision / Getty Images
Interior design by Dorie McClelland
The text of this book is set in Warnock Pro.
08 09 10 11 12 5 4 3 2 1
First Edition

Library of Congress Cataloging-in-Publication Data

Crabtree, Julie.
  Discovering pig magic / Julie Crabtree. — 1st ed.
      p. cm.
  Summary: After three sixth-grade best friends perform a "magic" ritual, they experience what they think are unintended consequences of their wishes and they must all find ways to deal with their lives—with or without magic.
  ISBN 978-1-57131-683-7 (hardcover : alk. paper) — ISBN 978-1-57131-684-4
(pbk. : alk. paper)
  [1. Best friends—Fiction. 2. Friendship—Fiction. 3. Magic—Fiction. 4. Schools—Fiction. 5. Alameda (Calif.)—Fiction.] I. Title.
  PZ7.C84152Di 2008
  [Fic]—dc22
                                    2008000625

This book is printed on acid-free, recycled (100 percent postconsumer waste) paper.

For Prince Phillip
and my little princesses,
Isabel and Charlotte

Sincerest thanks to Ben Barnhart, Allison Biggar, Mel Boring, Chere Irwin, Mom and Dad, Audrey, the Institute of Children's Literature, and Milkweed Editions. You are all part of this book's life.

Discovering Pig Magic

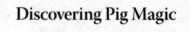

Discovering Pig Magic

Prologue
The Ritual

We dig the hole with our fingers. Grains of sand scrape our cuticles. Seagulls cry anxiously, spying on our secret work from above. When dirty bay water begins to ooze up from the bottom of the hole we stop digging. Nicki grabs the lined sheet of notebook paper and places it on her knee. Ariel and I remain silent. We have already decided Nicki's throaty voice will lend the reading power. We hold hands. Our dirt-streaked arms make a triangle frame around the scooped-out earth. We twine and tangle our hands together tightly, the sticks of our fingers pressing against each other. The black curtain of Nicki's hair fans in the wind as she clears her throat and begins.

I shall gather myself into myself again,
I shall take my scattered selves and make them one.
I shall fuse them into a polished crystal ball
Where I can see the moon and the flashing sun.
I shall sit like a sibyl, hour after hour intent.
Watching the future come and the present go—
And the little shifting pictures of people rushing
In tiny self-importance to and fro.

We each put our sacred thing into the hole then.
Ariel holds a tiny antique spoon in the palm of her
hand. The ancient silver winks in the sun as she rubs
its old-fashioned, curlicued handle. She holds it above
the hole and closes her eyes. The utensil makes a
dull, sticky sound when it hits the sludgy muck in the
hole. Next Nicki's thumb-sized leather doll joins the
spoon. The tiny, thread-bound figure clutches franti-
cally at a suede baby the size of a large pencil eraser.
The mother's turquoise eyes stare dully up into the sky.
Lastly, I bring forth my thing. My object of sacrifice.
The ceramic pig with real gold inlay plinks against the
spoon, and then rolls to the left of the mother and baby
figurine. I feel lighter, freer already.

Nicki squeezes my hand. I squeeze back.

"Did the book say how soon we would begin to see
the changes?" Ariel asked me.

"As soon as we've buried them I think. I don't know
for sure. The book didn't say exactly . . ."

After carefully refilling the hole with the sandy soil, we pack up in silence, thrilled and maybe even a little scared of the forces we have set in motion.

My Thirteenth Birthday
Brings No Surprises

I fix a smile on my face as Aunt Winda hands me the
package. It is small and heavy. The wrapping paper
has puffy tufts of white clouds floating over groups of
fat pink pigs. The pig smiles are so huge their eyes are
mere slits. I concentrate on ripping the paper through
the heads of the happy piggies. I succeed.

Aunt Winda, who teaches preschool, gives a little
hand clap of anticipation as I pick tape off the box.
I wonder what kind of pig this will be. Perhaps a
paperweight? No, I already have the pig-in-a-tutu
paperweight sitting on my desk. Another piggy bank?
No, I already have four. Maybe earrings? I don't have
pig-themed earrings yet, only a necklace with a little
sleeping piglet charm. Charming it is not. Wearing

pig jewelry is not exactly the road to popularity in the seventh grade.

At last I get through the deep folds of pig-pink tissue to find a fat plastic pig sprawling on her back, her stumpy legs in the air. Her huge stomach is studded with dark pink holes. It looks like she has strange, hollow nipples. Aunt Winda squeals.

"Can you believe it, Miss M? I found a pig pencil holder!"

"Wow, Aunt Winda." I hold up the strange animal.

My aunt grabs it from my hand and shoves it in my face. "And look, its little hooves are *magnets* . . . you know, to hold paper clips?"

"Thank you, Aunt Winda." I place the ugly thing on the table and try to look sincerely pleased.

"Well happy birthday, Miss M." Aunt Winda pats my arm. I nod and grab the next gift from the pile near my feet. I wonder what obnoxious pig things lurk in the other boxes. Smile plastered back in place, I rip into the closest package.

Just Call Me Pig Girl

I am lying on my bed listening to music. I am an only child with my own room, which I share with about a gazillion pigs. Thanks to the latest haul for my birthday today, it's a gazillion and three now. I hate pigs.

Let me explain. When I was four my parents took me to Iowa. My father had some sort of conference there, and my mother decided we would tag along and see "Middle America." We live in California. My mother always says living here, just outside San Francisco, is not really the "real" world. Frequently she'll point out things like organic food farmers' markets, paved bike paths, or our lesbian neighbors and tell me, "Where we live is different, it is not real America. It is better, freer. Not like other places."

I don't know how one place can be more or less real than another, but I don't question her anymore. And that's why, I imagine, she dragged me to Iowa . . . to see Un-California. Anyway, about the pigs.

The Iowa trip started the pig thing. While my father sat in meetings all day, my mother and I toured a farm. I was allowed to hold a tiny piglet in a sunny, hay-smelling barn. He had butted his adorable, scratchy head under my chin and squeaked endearingly. I was hooked. I rattled on about loving pigs on the plane ride home. Keep in mind I was in preschool at the time.

That year at Christmas I got flannel pajamas with little, purple, flying pigs on the collar and cuffs, a ceramic pig with a bunch of little piglets glued to her underbelly, and a Pig Chia Pet. I loved everything. My collection had begun.

The next year I started kindergarten. I still loved pigs. That year I got a bathroom set—complete with cup, toothbrush holder, and soap dispenser—patterned with pigs dancing. The set is on my bathroom counter right now. It says "cha-cha-cha" in gold, scrolling letters under each dancing pig trio. I wish I had the courage to break it.

By second grade I no longer liked pigs so much. I did not hate them, but I didn't want to collect them anymore either. That year my Aunt Winda found bed sheets with a pig pattern. Those pigs were strange, busy, people-like pigs. I had to sleep on top of pigs sipping coffee and gossiping, wearing overalls and carrying gardening shears, and baby pigs sitting on school benches staring at a chalkboard. Luckily for them, the overalls they wore all seemed to have custom-made pig-tail holes for comfort and convenience. Thankfully, the sheets wore out.

By third grade I hated pigs. I wish I had told everyone the truth about my feelings then. I didn't though, and the pig collection continued to grow. My family took great pride in finding rare, different, interesting, unique pig things for my collection. My father built shelves on my wall so I could display my pigs.

The pigs made everyone so happy, except me. I remember thinking I would bravely tell them all I hated pigs, but then my father left us. The timing seemed bad. My mother went out and bought me a Special Edition Babe DVD during our first week without dad around. I couldn't very well crush her, so I pretended to love it. I remember watching the outtakes with her several times in a row and forcing myself to pretend to enjoy them. And so it has gone on.

I am in seventh grade now, and I have what might possibly be the largest collection of pig stuff on the planet. You'd be surprised how many pig-themed things there are once you start looking. I wish my room would somehow catch on fire and burn it all. Bacon!

I can't have anyone from school over here. Well, not anyone new I mean (except Nicki and Ariel, of course). Junior high is like the same school, because everyone I've known forever from elementary school is there, but also like a new school. The other elementary schools are there too. Kids I don't know. Boys I haven't met. I feel like now more than ever before, these pigs could really embarrass me . . . stop me from ever starting a better social life.

Can you imagine it? If they knew I had all these various pigs. . . . I hate to think of the possibilities, given the talent and creativity of the junior high population. I could be called pig girl. Even though I'm not fat, kids might wonder what I have in common with the animal. They would find similarities. And really, it is just a *childish* collection. My old friends from elementary school know about it (the few I'd become friends with); they've watched the collection grow over the years, but they don't care. Junior high is different. I have a chance to start fresh, sort of. . . . I do not want to become known for pigs.

What Is My Name?

I am digging in the freezer, trying to find chocolate-chip toaster waffles. I have exactly ten minutes to eat breakfast and brush my teeth before we leave for school. My mom comes in the kitchen, yawning.

"Morning, Miss M." She kisses my cheek. Her ancient slippers thwack the kitchen tiles as she crosses to the coffee maker. I hear her give a little huff of satisfaction that this morning the temperamental timer has worked and the coffee is ready.

"Hi, Mom. Are we out of toaster waffles?"

She sips her coffee, leans against the counter, thinking.

"If you finished 'em, we're out."

This is such a mom response. She is not what you would call a morning person. Her sarcasm is typical. I give up and grab the box of Honey Nut Cheerios. Mom disappears down the hall, presumably to throw on sweats and a T-shirt.

She works from our "home office," which is basically the corner of the dining room where the computer and a small table are crammed. Mom does medical billing for hospitals and insurance companies. Working at home allows her to be slobby most of the time. She drops me off at school without getting out of the car, comes home and works, and I walk home after school with my two best friends. Except for going grocery shopping and doing errands, Mom doesn't leave the house much.

I finish my cereal quickly. I brush my teeth with the whitening toothpaste which, it turns out, works wonders on killing a pimple. The secret is to put the toothpaste on the zit while it's just a little underground sore spot, not yet risen and red. Today I think my skin looks pretty okay, and my hair even looks decent. I have what I think of as honey-colored hair on my good days and mouse-brown hair on my bad days.

Mom and I head out to the car. I am pleased to see my mother has, indeed, replaced her nightgown and bathrobe with actual clothes, even though the loose cotton is baggy and dung colored. She used to stay in her nightgown to drop me off. She said it was a waste of time to get dressed when she never had to get out of the car. Then, a few months ago, another car rear-ended our ancient Volvo. Mom had to get out of the car in her faded, oversized Pooh Bear nightshirt and ratty slippers to exchange insurance papers and all that. Everyone in the school must have seen her. Since then, she has thrown on "real" clothes before we go.

"Anything going on in school today?" she asks as she backs the old car down the driveway.

"No, not really." I fiddle with the buttons on my shirt. I got two new shirts from the Gap Outlet for my birthday. Amazingly, they do not have any pigs on them.

"Your new shirt looks good, Miss M. You got a good haul yesterday for your birthday, eh?"

I think of the pig pencil holder and say nothing. We pull into the school lot and wait in a long line of cars, creeping toward the drop-off zone. If you try to jump out of the car before it's officially in the zone marked with pylons, Miss Reed will yell at you and reprimand your parent. Miss Reed is our history teacher. She takes safety very seriously.

I grab my backpack and pop my seatbelt as we glide between the orange cones. I see Ariel, my best friend, getting out of her dad's silver Suburban ahead of us. Mom turns her cheek toward me for a kiss, as she does every morning.

"Bye, *Matilda*," she says with emphasis. "Have a good day."

I peck her cheek and scramble out, slamming the door. I wish she wouldn't make such a big deal about the Matilda thing.

Let me explain. I didn't go to Aunt Winda's pre-school, but I visited her there a couple times when I was little. Apparently I heard the kids calling her *Miss* Winda. I have no memory of this, but both my aunt and my mother have told me the story thousands of times. Anyway, they say I thought it sounded glamorous or something. I demanded that everyone start calling me *Miss* Matilda. They all thought it was hilarious and shortened it to Miss M. My mom, aunt, their friends, and even some of mine still call me that. My dad is the only one who has always called me Matilda. I only see him a couple times a year now though, so it doesn't count.

I never really minded being Miss M until this year. When I started middle school I thought it would be easy to make a clean break from the nickname. I asked everyone to stop calling me Miss M. I decided Mattie was cute, but Mom said she wouldn't substitute one nickname for another, and I'd have to settle for Matilda. I introduced myself as Mattie to everyone at the new school. A few weeks into the school year Ariel called me Miss M at lunch in front of the whole cafeteria. Of course, it immediately stuck again.

Now everyone just calls me "M." I actually like it. It seems like a small, neat thing to be called a letter. It makes me feel liked somehow.

As I approach the front entrance, I think about the

way I have become a pig collector even though I don't want to be and the fact that one comment I made when I was three years old created a nickname I can't shake. It is scary that stuff we say and do, even as tiny kids, can keep influencing our lives so much.

Meet My Two Best Friends

I am walking home with Ariel and Nicki. We live within a few blocks of each other. Ariel and I have been friends since we were in kindergarten. Nicki just moved to Alameda this year. Somehow she just instantly fit with us. It started in our homeroom when Nicki sat between Ariel and me. She passed notes for us, got caught, and when she took detention instead of telling the teacher on me and Ariel we knew she was special. Since then, we have become our own little unit of three. And since performing the ritual by the bay, with our sacred objects, we are even more connected to one another.

Ariel has had to fight the Little Mermaid jokes her whole life. Her red hair is cut very short for obvious reasons. And let me mention, it is not a coincidence that Ariel has red hair . . . her mother named her after

THE Disney Ariel. On purpose. Ariel wants to bleach it blonde, to distance herself from the ditzy mermaid, but her mother won't let her until high school.

Junior high has brought Ariel a fresh batch of name humor. Boys make comments about her "shells" and "tail." Ariel does have an impressive chest for a seventh grader, which mostly embarrasses her. If she'd stop wearing hugely baggy shirts and grow her hair, she really could look like Ariel. I mean that as a compliment. But she hates her hair and her boobs. She says boys and social climbing are "counterproductive to her cooking." More on that later . . .

Nicki is half Native American. She is an actual American Indian (well half), which most people find fascinating. She grew up in a small town in central California called North Fork. Nicki's Native American side of the family is still there, and she misses them. Nicki's family moved here this year because her dad got a forest service job close by. Her mom doesn't work because she stays home with Nicki's new baby brother.

Nicki has smooth, black hair that looks like shiny water running down her back. Her eyes are blue though, like her father's. She looks exotic. She is really shy, and so far only Ariel and I have become her friends. It works for all of us, this trio.

Right now Ariel is telling us about some recipe she wants to try this weekend. Ariel is obsessed with cooking. She watches cooking shows constantly.

Unlike most of us, she knows exactly what she wants to do with her life: Be A Famous Chef. She brings little Tupperware containers to school sometimes with dishes that have been emulsified, reduced, caramelized, or brined. While a few of her dishes have gone wrong, most are delicious.

"So if you guys want to come over Saturday, maybe early in the afternoon, you could quiz me for the history test while I make it, and then stay for dinner . . ." Ariel leaves the question in the air. She knows we are hesitant.

Nicki answers first. "As long as it doesn't have any of that, what was it . . . that intestine stuff, in it?" She shudders a bit in memory.

"That was chitterlings. I told you, that was a southern meal. They're popular in the South." Ariel takes another breath to continue her speech, and I jump in.

"But we're from California, and we don't eat intestines." Nicki high-fives me from the side. Ariel just sighs.

"This time it's Italian, guys. You know . . . pasta, veal, tomatoes . . ."

"No veal!" Nicki shakes her head as she walks. "They put baby cows in dark boxes and tie them up to make veal."

"Fine, I'll use ground beef," Ariel sounds sulky, "or maybe ground pork." She pauses and looks at me sideways, a gleam in her eye. "Or will eating your little piggy friends be upsetting?"

Ariel is allowed to tease me about the pigs because there is no meanness in it with her. I laugh and playfully punch her upper arm.

"Okay, Ariel, I'll come. But we really do have to study for history and not just gossip while you're cooking."

"Good plan," Nicki says, "but no veal."

"Yeah whatever, no veal. I just hope the béchamel sauce will bind ground beef."

Nicki and I shoot each other little smiles over Ariel's scruffy red head. We have arrived at Nicki's street. She crosses and heads toward her house. We wave. We have never been in Nicki's house, never been invited. Ariel and I continue walking, heading toward our own homes.

My Mother Is a Computer Addict

Saturday dawns foggy and gray. Alameda sits right on the San Francisco Bay and is often overcast like this. It depresses me sometimes. I linger in bed too long and am shocked to see that it is already after ten. I throw a sweatshirt over my rumpled sleep tank and head to the kitchen. The familiar smell of coffee cuts the air. Mom is at the computer playing Zoo Tycoon.

"Hey, Mom." I stretch, going up on my toes and arching my back until my spine makes little, crunchy, popping noises. Feels good. "Can I have a cup of coffee?"

She doesn't turn away from the game as she answers, "One cup, Miss M." I see her move a panda bear. "Plans today?" She pauses the game and swivels her chair to look at me.

"Nicki and I are going to Ariel's later on. That okay?"

"Isn't the big history test on Monday?"

"Yeah, it is. We're studying for it today. While Ariel cooks."

Mom nods. She knows all about Ariel's cooking. In fact, I usually bring home leftovers. I think it gives Mom a nice break from her usual dinners of Lean Cuisine. She also knows that I will do fine on the history test. I am what adults call "self-motivated" about school. Basically, I get good grades without threat or reward.

"Okay, sounds fun. Bring me a plate?" I feel a pang of guilt suddenly. Lately, Mom has seemed so . . . defeated. All she does is work or play on the computer. Even Aunt Winda hasn't been around so much lately.

"Sure. And maybe we could watch a late movie or something when I get home?"

She has already turned back to her game. She mumbles something about needing another bathroom for her zoo. She doesn't answer.

Mrs. Rosencrantz's Sneak Attack

Ariel is twirling batter around a hot skillet. Nicki and I sit on bar stools at the counter, watching. Ariel is wearing a professional-looking, crisp, white apron her mother bought her for Christmas. It wraps around her tiny body completely. Her enviable chest makes an unexpected mound beneath the rectangular straps. She looks like a strange, top-heavy, red-capped mummy.

Nicki is supposed to be quizzing Ariel and me on the American Revolution. Instead, we are talking about Mrs. Rosencrantz. Mrs. Rosencrantz is Ariel's neighbor, and if you are unlucky enough to cross paths with her, she will talk and talk. You will find yourself backing away, edging down the sidewalk, and she will follow. In her high-pitched, old-lady voice, she'll go on and on about how Alameda used to be when the naval base was thriving. She is desperate and eager to converse, and it is maddening. In fact, she trapped me today. I had been daydreaming, walking along, and didn't notice her weeding the sidewalk between her house and Ariel's.

"I hate how she always says 'the island' when she talks about Alameda," Nicki says.

"At least you guys don't have to live by her. She tries to catch me after school all the time." Ariel expertly slides a paper-thin crepe onto a sheaf of waiting wax paper and flicks a dab of butter into the pan. It sizzles and the smell of browned butter settles over us. I feel cozy and happy with the butter smell hanging in the air.

"I mean I know she's lonely, being a widow and all, but geez, she practically attacks people . . ." Ariel pours a dollar-sized puddle of batter into the hot pan. She quickly lifts it from the burner and tilts the pan around in circles, creating what looks like a skin.

"I thought we were getting *Italian* food, Ariel." I am tired of talking about Mrs. Rosencrantz. "I am pretty sure crepes are French."

"These are called *crespelle* in Italian cooking. They are crepes, but not French."

"Oh." I don't really care, but at least the subject has changed.

Nicki thwacks the open history book with her palm, making a "come-to-attention" sound. "Let's do fifteen minutes of quizzing without interrupting ourselves."

Ariel and I both murmur agreement.

Nicki clears her throat. "How many colonies were there under British rule when the war began?"

Ariel and I both chant "thirteen."

Nicki continues, and we buckle down to study. We get through about half the chapter when Ariel's mom and brother burst through the door. Her brother ignores us as always and we hear his door slam down the hall. He's fifteen.

"Hi, girls!" Ariel's mom gives us a little wave. "Smells good, honey," she says to Ariel as she kisses her head. "I was going to garden a bit, but Mrs. Rosencrantz is out there."

We all burst out laughing.

Mom Tries Too Hard to Bond with Me

It's Sunday evening. Mom and I are eating leftovers I brought home from Ariel's yesterday. The dish is rich and delicate, flavored strongly with nutmeg. We are eating off the same plate, sitting side by side on the floor in front of the low-slung coffee table, and watching the movie *Big* on TV. Mom seems totally engrossed in it, but it's boring. The hairstyles are puffy and carefully placed. So eighties.

"Miss M," Mom says (it sounds like "missum" the way she says it), "you're going to love this part. It is so funny."

I hate it when she makes comments about what's coming up in a movie, telling me how I will react to it. I purposely remain stony faced as Tom Hanks makes fake little-boy gestures, ignorant to the sexiness of the woman. Mom laughs out loud, and tiny speckles of Ariel's béchamel sauce fly out of her mouth. It is disgusting.

"I'm going to my room."

Mom looks up at me. Her eyes look wounded. "Don't you want to finish watching this movie?" She pauses, takes a bite, and watches me. "With me?"

"No, I'm full, and I need to finish up a couple pages of math." I stand up.

"Oh, okay, honey." She sounds disappointed, but I ignore it. I head to my room. I am so ready for things to change around here.

The Sacred Objects Work Their Magic (I Think James Likes Me!)

I am so glad it's Friday. Sometimes the week seems unending, especially when Ariel isn't around. She missed school all week because she got strep throat. Nicki and I hung out, but it's not the same without Ariel.

My dad is coming to visit tomorrow. He lives in Sacramento now, which is about two hours, in traffic, from Alameda. When he moved there two years ago he promised he'd be back a lot to visit, but it hasn't happened that way. I have only visited him once. I like staying back here at home. It was awkward and boring staying with him in the apartment he rents.

On Fridays our school gets out right after lunch. Usually Ariel, Nicki, and I take a walk along the meandering trail that loops around Bay Farm Island. On clear days the bay sparkles like a giant, placid lake. San

Francisco looks close enough to touch, the buildings appearing to rise out of the water. We usually sit in the scrappy grass along the trail when we are tired of walking, and talk. Some of our deepest talks have taken place along that path. Sitting, staring out at the draping cables holding up the Bay Bridge or meditating on the rolling humps of the Marin Headlands, we are three girls against the world. We did the magic here, but we haven't talked about it. We might weaken its potential with words.

I start thinking about it. The book. With its cracked purple cover and colorful swirls. It had been buried under a pile of cheap novels at a sidewalk sale. Its title was impossible to read at first because of the ornate design. Then, like one of those posters you must stare at without blinking to see the "hidden" picture in, I suddenly saw the title clearly: *The Natural World: Magic.* The spine had cracked when I opened it, as though it had been closed for a very long time. A smell like damp dirt and ripe fruit had risen from its thick, brittle pages. I bought it. I thought it would be interesting, nothing more. I didn't believe in magic, of course. But that's changed.

The three of us pored over the book. We had discovered a history book of ancient magic. Witchcraft, spells, runes, it's all been around forever. There is evidence, even a few blurry pictures of people from long ago doing their rituals. The book is also an instruction manual. It warns the reader to use GREAT care when conjuring the ancient magic.

We all agree that finding the book, or the book finding us, was no accident. It seems silly to believe in magic perhaps, but anyone who reads this book with an open mind would be forced to reconsider. The timing was perfect too. There are no coincidences, no accidents. That's another thing the book teaches.

We all hoped the start of seventh grade would be a new beginning. We had followed the instructions exactly. The objects, the place near water, the beautiful poem "The Crystal Gazer" by Sara Teasdale I found in a poetry book of my mom's . . . every element of the ritual had been performed. We all felt awed, hopeful, and even a bit scared that day. We had worked together, pushing the sloppy piles of sandy mud back into the hole without talking.

Our sacred objects are buried along the path we are walking now, but we still never speak of them. I don't need to ask to know that Nicki and Ariel think about them like I do all the time. I know we all feel the electricity that came to life among us that day.

I focus on the landscape around me as I think about the ritual. I can't remember anymore which tree marks the spot. I think I might remember, if I look hard at each clump of trees, how the branches were shaped. I know they were strangely twisted around each other. There is so much wind and water assaulting the trees along here that many of them are crooked and hunching, warped into odd formations, so it might be hard to find the exact location. We should have marked the place somehow, but it's too late now.

I wish sometimes I could dig them up, the "objects" (that's what the book said to call them). The gold on the pig my dad gave me when I turned ten is probably disappearing into the gritty sand. I picture Nicki's Indian mother and baby weeping and choking in the sealed earth. Ariel's spoon is probably dull and lusterless by now. I feel the raw power three girls can create, have created, and sometimes I feel scared.

I think we all feel the momentum of our lives picking up speed, going toward something. We know it is the objects, the ritual we performed months ago, that has created this sense of motion. That's why we can't speak of it, we are frightened that words might halt or damage what has been begun. I don't know if Ariel and Nicki feel like I do, but they too are silent about the secret buried things, so I think they must.

Today Nicki and I decide to walk the trail together without Ariel. This is a first. Nicki is quiet. Usually she is content to listen to Ariel and me on this walk, only adding into the conversation now and then. I suddenly realize that as well as the three of us get along, there's still a lot I don't know about Nicki.

The air is damp and chilly as we head across the

footbridge that connects Alameda's main island to Bay Farm Island. The bay is flat gray. It reminds me of my mom. We cannot see San Francisco today but we know it is there, shrouded in wet fog. Nicki is walking in front of me. Little droplets cling to her black hair. She looks bejeweled.

"Do you miss North Fork?" I ask her.

"Not really. Well, I miss my cousins."

I nod, but she can't see me because I am walking behind her. She doesn't say anything else.

"My dad is coming tomorrow," I tell her.

"Are you glad?"

I consider the question. My Skechers make a thud-scrape rhythm as I walk and it sounds like "glad-dad-glad-dad" in my mind.

"It's fine. He wants to give me my birthday present in person. Then we're going to eat dinner at El Sombrero."

Nicki stops, picks up a flattish stone and pitches it into the bay. A bright red and blue Southwest plane flies low over our heads. Its engines vibrate the ground and block out the plopping sound Nicki's stone must have made. We stop talking automatically. The Oakland Airport is on the end of Bay Farm Island, so low-flying planes are an ever-present part of our walks.

The plane's rumble fades. We have come to our usual sitting spot. I sit. Nicki sits too. I feel sad on this gray day, missing Ariel and wondering if I am glad to see my father.

Nicki picks up the thread of our conversation. "Do your mom and him . . . your dad . . . get along? I mean . . . since the divorce?"

"They do actually." It's something surprising to people, that divorced people can be friendly. "The three of us—me and my mom and dad—are eating out there tomorrow. We used to eat there every Saturday, when he lived with us." This is a useless fact and I don't know why I have told it to Nicki.

"Cool." Nicki smiles suddenly.

"What?" I ask her.

"Do you think the present your dad's bringing will, oh, 'oink'?" She gives me a little push on the shoulder.

I roll me eyes, sigh with exaggerated drama. "God, please, no more pigs." I clench my hands and wring them as though the world is ending. Nicki laughs.

"Let's head back, I'm cold."

Nicki nods. "Mattie?" (She is the only one left who calls me Mattie, and I feel a rush of warmth toward her because of it.)

"Yeah?"

"James has a crush on you." She says it in a secretive tone.

"Shut up! How do you know?"

Nicki smiles like the Mona Lisa. "Dustin heard it from his little sister. She's James's sister's best friend."

"And you waited till *now* to tell me?" I grab a wad of damp black hair and give it a playful tug. "How could you? I mean . . . *James!*" James is an official hottie. I have had a crush on him since school started.

"I was waiting until it was a good time. You seemed kind of down, and it cheered you up, right?"

That is a gross understatement. I might possibly levitate.

"And also, well, it is such a rumor. You know, coming from James's little sister. And even then, it came from Dustin's sister first . . . she's kind of gossipy . . ." Nicki trails off and gives me a look that says *don't get your hopes up too much.*

But they're way up. Suddenly having my dad visit, knowing I will probably get another pig from him, doesn't seem so depressing. Going home to my mom in her gray clothes playing Zoo Tycoon doesn't seem so awful either. Even a slight possibility that James likes me is enough. Right now, it's enough.

We chatter along back across the foot bridge. There is a cloud break just above the city, and I can see the sharp angle of the Transamerica Building peeking out. I feel like my mood change has somehow influenced the weather and created that little pocket of sunshine.

Dad Visits

Dad shows up right on time, like always. He comes in and comments on how great everything looks in the house (even though it's a mess . . . the living room paint is peeling next to the window, and one of the blinds is stuck permanently up at a crooked angle). Mom hasn't bothered to change her baggy T-shirt, though she is wearing mascara at least. Dad and Mom sit at the kitchen table and look at papers for awhile—something to do with health insurance for me—then we leave for dinner.

Alameda is flat and everything's close together, so walking places is common when you live here. El Sombrero is within easy walking distance of our house. Before the divorce, we used to walk here together every Saturday. After dinner we would walk down Park Street, past the little mall, and all the way to the bay's edge. I loved our Saturday walks.

The walk tonight is silent and the old feeling of family is totally gone. We walk quickly to get there. My mom walks slightly ahead of us. She is obviously uncomfortable being outside. I realize she's lost weight. The poky parts of her spine show when the wind presses the T-shirt against her back.

I order cheese enchiladas and a Dr. Pepper, as usual. Dad asks me about school, about Ariel, about my pig collection. I answer everything with no-meaning words like "good" and "fine." Mom sits by politely. She drinks a margarita and plays with her chile relleno, peeling little bits of soggy breading in careful strips.

I eat quickly. Mom is telling dad about a strange insurance issue she's working on. She mentions "polyps" several times, and it is making me feel queasy. The word conjures up an image of ripe, grapelike clusters pulsing with blood. My enchilada suddenly seems suspect.

"Mom, enough with the disease talk."

She laughs, nods her head. "Sorry, honey."

Dad clears his throat. "Well, Matilda, looks like we're all done eating anyway." He pushes his plate away. "You ready for your present?"

"Okay, dad." I crumple my napkin and throw it on my plate. It instantly bonds with the leftover rubbery cheese. Ariel's enchiladas have some sort of dryish, crumbly cheese in them that is much better than this plastic cheese El Sombrero uses.

Dad reaches into his brown leather satchel and

brings out a wrapped square. He hands it to me, smiling with expectation.

"Thanks, Dad."

"Well wait and see what it is before you thank me." He winks.

The wrapping paper says "Happy Birthday" in that kind of writing that is supposed to look like some adorable kindergartner wrote it . . . the letters all blocky and carefully irregular. It is way too young for me. It annoys me and makes me really sad all at once that Dad would choose it for me. It is wrapped with such perfection I can tell he must have had the store wrap it for him. He had looked at those rolls they have behind the gift-wrap counter and pointed at *this* pattern. The paper gives me a gloomy sense of doom about the present. The man still thinks I'm seven years old.

I can tell from the shape and size that it's some sort of picture. I shred through the paper and it is, all right. I stare at it numbly. I will have to hang it on my wall. Oh god, it is the most hideous thing I have ever laid eyes on.

"It's an original, Matilda. Look, it's *signed!*" Dad grabs the picture from me, jabs his finger at the corner. "I found it in a gallery in Old Sacramento. You know, by that kite shop?"

"Wow, Dad . . . it's . . . unique." I try to sound thrilled. He buys it. Mom tips back in her chair and watches people walking by, seemingly unaware of the monstrosity I have just received.

"I knew you'd love it." Dad huffs breath on a non-existent speck on the glass and rubs it with his shirt. "I'll help you mount it in your room before I leave."

He hands the picture back to me. "Great, Dad." I smile with my lips closed. I would love to drop it and watch it shatter on the ugly, stained restaurant carpet, but Dad would just get it reframed.

I stare again at the picture. The pig face is done in charcoal. The pig looks wise and serious, as though while he posed for his portrait to be painted he was considering various solutions for world peace. He wears a bow tie. His head is tilted slightly to one side, and he has a little trimmed goatee. My god, it is the ugliest, strangest "art" I have seen.

We walk home directly. No more walks out to the bay. Dad hangs the picture for me on the wall across from my bed. He makes a great show of leveling it. After Dad leaves I take it down and slide it under my bed. I'll put it up on days he comes. I call Ariel. I tell her about the picture and she cracks up. It makes me feel better.

We talk about James after that. She thinks he wears hair gel. I think his hair's naturally well shaped. We agree to meet up tomorrow for a picnic lunch on the Bay Farm Island Trail. Nicki can meet us too.

I dream about a pig with a bow tie teaching algebra while James makes paper cut-out snowflake chains at a child's desk in front of me. He hands the beautiful strings of connected snowflakes to me, and I eat them.

Mom Has a Date!

It is late afternoon, and I have just come back from a long and windy walk with Ariel and Nicki. My cheeks are raw from the whip of wind and my lips are chapped from licking them over and over. I am full of my friends' secrets and purged of my own. I feel tired and pleasant.

Aunt Winda's Toyota Prius is parked at the curb by our house. She doesn't usually come over on Sundays, but I am happy she's here. I slam the door to announce myself.

Aunt Winda's voice yells from the back of the house, "We're back here, Miss M!" She sounds very far away, though she can't be. Our house, like so many in Alameda, is a long, narrow affair built seventy-five years ago. From the street it looks tiny, but inside it's big. Or, I should say, long. The shape has advantages—

I can blast the TV and Mom doesn't hear it in her bedroom.

I throw my bag down and go see what they're up to. The door to Mom's room is wide open and there is a black platform shoe I don't recognize on its side in the doorway.

Aunt Winda yanks me into the room. "Doesn't she look fabulous?"

My mother smiles at me lopsidedly and brushes nervously at the dark green skirt she's wearing. The outfit is new or borrowed; I haven't seen it before. She wears a crisp white shirt with extra-large cuffs and buttons made to look like pearls. The outfit makes her look like a teacher or a secretary or something. That aside, I am thrilled to see her away from the computer, showered, blow-dried, and dressed, so I tell her, "Rock on, Mom!"

"She has a date, Miss M!" My Aunt fussily pats my mother's freshly curled hair.

"With who?" I am pleased I manage to sound so casual with this news. My mother has not dated since my father left. I don't want to jinx it by acting nervous or hyper or something. I can feel my mother's eyes watching me too closely. I flop on her bed and continue my bored routine.

"A divorced dad from the preschool." Aunt Winda winks at my mother. "And just let me say, *hubba hubba.*"

I groan. "Aunt Winda, *'hubba hubba'?*" I shake my head at her dinosaur language.

"It means he's cute, little Miss *Teenager.*"

I laugh. I haven't been a teenager very long, and I am secretly happy that Aunt Winda is acknowledging my new status. I still feel twelve, I guess. "I know that Auntie. It just sounds so . . . *old* or something."

My mother and Aunt Winda giggle at each other. I can tell Mom is nervous, but happy too.

"He just called today, while you were gone, M." Mom is picking the cuticle on her index finger as she speaks. "Winda gave him my number last week. I mean I said it was okay . . ." Mom gives Winda a nod. "Well, anyway, he called while you were out with your friends. I didn't think he would actually ever call." She shrugs, shakes her head, continues. "He got tickets, last minute, to that play at the Orpheum. I said it sounded fun." As she says the word "fun" the little strip of cuticle skin she's been ripping and picking gives way. I see her wince slightly. She puts the injured finger in her mouth.

Aunt Winda beams. "And I'll stay here tonight, Miss M, because your mother may be back pretty late. She raises her eyebrows at Mom, and Mom sticks her tongue out in response. And *I* am the kid around here?

I yawn, acting like this whole date thing is routine, common, expected. "Great. Sounds fun, Mom." I hop off the bed. "I'm going to go to my room. Listen to music." I yawn again (am I overdoing it?) to show how calm and unaffected I am.

I slouch out of the bedroom. Just before I close my bedroom door I hear my mother and Aunt Winda whispering something about me "taking it well." I can't believe they would worry. I think Mom dating is fantastic.

The Date Disaster

I fell asleep on the couch last night watching TV. I tried to stay up—I really wanted to hear about the date. Aunt Winda went to bed at ten o'clock and told me not to wait up, but I think she knew I would. I made it until almost two o'clock in the morning, when I finally gave up and went to bed. My alarm blares at six thirty, and I am still exhausted. I force myself out of bed.

I hear Aunt Winda's voice coming from the kitchen. I head that way, hoping I can convince Mom to let me have some coffee. Staying awake in school is going to be major torture without a little help. Aunt Winda is making muffins from a mix. Mom is already on the computer. She's playing Mall Tycoon this morning.

Aunt Winda greets me first. "Morning, Miss M!" She is too loud and cheerful.

My mother pauses her game and gives me a little wave, but doesn't look up for more than two seconds.

Her face is blotchy and swollen around the eyes. Her lips look scabbed and dry.

"Hi, honey. Look, Winda's making muffins!" She sounds so thrilled about muffins from a box, it is ridiculous.

I want to ask about the date, but I don't. Mom looks like hell. No one mentions it. I hate this tension. I leave, go back to my room.

Aunt Winda appears in my doorway. "The guy was a jerk, Miss M." She comes over and sits on the edge of my bed. She picks up the corkscrew pigtail bookmark she gave me in my stocking last year. She turns it over and over as she speaks. "I could kill that guy!" She bends the bookmark into a rainbow. That'll ruin it for sure, which is fine with me.

"He said he wasn't ready, really, yet, to see anyone. He thought he was, but after dinner he sort of had second thoughts or something." The bookmark is starting to tear at the crease Aunt Winda is making. She doesn't seem to notice. I dig in my drawer for clean socks that match and wait to hear more.

"He told her it wasn't *her* and all that . . ."—Aunt Winda sounds really mad now—"and of course it really *wasn't*. I mean your Mom is pretty, smart . . ." I can tell Aunt Winda feels like this is all her fault. I can tell she wants to kill the guy.

"Wow. That stinks. Should I go talk to Mom?"

"Maybe after school, honey. She asked me to tell

you what happened, give her some space." Aunt Winda shakes her head. "I think she's okay. I just can't believe he did this to her . . . her first date and the guy makes her feel rejected like that! And get this . . . he asked her if she still wanted to see the play, and she said yes! He went home. She went to the Orpheum alone."

This bit of information, more than anything else, makes me hurt for my mother. I picture her smoothing the green skirt over her knees and setting her purse in the vacant seat next to her. I see her sitting there in the half dark, alone, staring ahead.

"I have to get dressed, Aunt Winda." I pull her arm so she'll get off my bed.

"Oh, yeah, okay." She drops the ruined bookmark on my bedspread. "Grab a muffin on your way out if you want."

"Thanks." I close the door and face my closet. Today I will talk to James. I am determined. What to wear, what to wear? It soothes me to concentrate on clothes. I don't want to think about Mom's date disaster.

On the way to school Mom is silent, distracted. I feel like I am going to explode with anticipation about James. I just can't feel sad for Mom right now. I see Nicki up ahead, and after kissing Mom on the cheek, I run to meet her. I am relieved when the Volvo disappears from sight.

I Want to Die

It is the Saturday before Thanksgiving. We are all going
to Ariel's house for a sushi feast. Her birthday was last
week, and her mom got her a sushi-making kit. Now
two of the three of us are officially teenagers.

At first I said I was too depressed to go anywhere,
but Nicki talked me into coming. She guilted me
about hurting Ariel's feelings. Truthfully, I am looking
forward to getting out of the house. I just don't want
to talk about the James thing anymore. Nicki promised
me they wouldn't bring it up.

It happened three days ago, and I still want to die. I
should have known not to believe rumors. When Nicki
told me she had heard James liked me, well, I really
wanted to think it was true. Plus, Nicki is not the gossiping, exaggerating kind at all, so it seemed believable

coming from her. Thinking back, I know Nicki was careful to say it was one of those passed-down things she'd heard, that I shouldn't get too excited. But I did.

James seemed extra friendly to me all last week. With my secret knowledge that he returned my feelings, I saw signs of proof. I thought he was smiling at me more. In pre-algebra he picked up my backpack for me when it fell off the hook in the back of the room. Then, last Thursday at lunch, he sat two people away from us on the picnic bench by the science building. It seemed so obvious to me that the rumor was true. I am such a moron. I can see now that I was looking too hard for signs that didn't really exist.

I did have one really happy week though, thinking that way. Every night, while mom squinted at the computer and muttered about her zoo or her mall (she's been tycooning nonstop since the date disaster), I colored and doodled in my journal and thought about James. I couldn't wait for him to finally talk to me, see if I wanted to go out with him.

I had pictured us holding hands and walking along the bay. The golden honey color hidden in my hair would glint in the sun. We would talk, and he would be amazed by my intelligence and wit. He would casually drape an arm across my shoulder, and I would gently lean into him, letting him know I felt the same way.

I spent hours on the phone with Ariel and Nicki,

planning my future with James. Tickets for the winter dance would go on sale Friday, and I was sure James would ask me.

By Wednesday he hadn't asked. I thought he must be working up the courage. Ariel and Nicki convinced me to sit by him at lunch that day. Clare Montgomery was sitting next to him already, so I sat across. Clare smiled at me. She looked older than seventh grade with her tight shirt and exposed stomach. Clare has always been the slutty-looking girl in our class. In junior high there are other girls like her from other schools . . . she's what Ariel calls "a type." They walk around in a pack and all the boys stare at them.

Anyway, when I sat down, James said hey. Clare started talking about spray-on tans. I tried to catch James's eye, to roll my own at Clare's silly topic, but he seemed to be listening intently. That should have clued me in, but it didn't. Clare stopped talking to stuff Cheetos in her mouth, and James turned to me.

"You going to the winter dance?" Finally, he would ask!

I had kept myself calm, taking a small bite of my sandwich and shaking my head casually. I *felt* quite calm. After all, I knew he would ask. I was unsurprised.

I waited for him to go on. Clare sucked Cheeto goo off her fingers loudly, and James slid his eyes back to her and watched her insert each red-tipped, ringed finger into her mouth. Eew.

I thought he must be having a hard time asking.

Poor guy. Clare was so disgusting, making those sucking sounds.

I couldn't stand it. "Are you asking me to the dance James?" Obviously he was. I tried to sound flirty and fun.

Clare choked on purpose right then, and a little spray of nasty, chewed Cheetos hit the table. "You're *serious?*" She shook her head slightly, took a swig of her Diet Coke. She swung her hair off her shoulder and pursed her over-glossed lips in delight.

James looked down at the table, mute.

"Sorry M." Clare swished Diet Coke through her teeth and swallowed loudly before continuing. "James and I are going. That's why I'm getting the spray-on tan. For my strapless dress. Weren't you listening?" She shook her head in pity.

All I could hear was a buzzing in my brain. James started to say something, but I was already up. Clare told him to let me go, laughing a little. I walked to the bathroom in a trance. The humiliation was so intense it made me literally dizzy. I really do wish I had died right then.

Nicki and Ariel better keep their promise today. I am talked out about this whole thing. I lay in bed last night and tried to figure out where to go from here. At home things are a mess. Mom never leaves the house except to drop me off in the morning at school. She plays Tycoon games all day and night. I can't talk to her. Dad hasn't even been making his weekly call lately. And now my social life is destroyed. I can't make eye contact with anyone at school after making such a fool of myself.

Everything is changing, but in terrible ways. It's because we buried those objects. That's what I thought of last night. We need to dig them up. I am going to tell Nicki and Ariel we have to do it. We'll eat sushi and figure out how to reverse the ritual.

Ariel's in Supersize Trouble

We each have a little bamboo mat. Ariel is laying out deep red, square ceramic plates with seaweed, rice, avocados, flaky white meat, and slices of something that looks like thin, pink plastic. It grosses me out, but I don't say anything. *Everyone* eats sushi in the Bay Area and I always act like I love it, but secretly some of it seems nasty to me. Also, Ariel can be very sensitive about her cooking. In fact, all three of us seem touchy today.

"Now use the seaweed as the wrapper." Ariel is using her teaching tone, which is annoying, but we are used to it. She passes me the rice. "Put that on next, M, in a thin layer."

I obey. The sticky grains won't come off my fingers. I shake them and little white globs sail through the air and land in Nicki's hair. Nicki picks the rice out of her hair and eats it. I laugh.

Ariel slams down a bowl and turns away from us, angrily wiping the already-clean tile counter.

"Geez, Ariel, chill. Sorry. It is *sticky* rice, you were right." I am trying to snap her out of whatever funk she's in, but she just shakes her head without looking up. We hardly ever argue and sulk when we're together. I don't like this.

"What is UP?" I ask, annoyed. I am the injured one here, having been publicly humiliated. Why is *Ariel* being so dramatic?

Ariel begins to cry. I feel instantly guilty. Ariel never cries.

"Air, are you okay?" Nicki pushes aside her bamboo mat, spilling a sloppy pile of fake crab and avocado, and touches Ariel's arm.

Ariel turns to us. Her apron is stained with soy sauce and there is a an unidentifiable streak of something green on her arm. Her red hair sticks up lopsidedly and her face is turning blotchy and puffed like poked-at Silly Putty. She looks young to me. The huge shelf of her chest doesn't match the rest of her.

"I am in sooo much trouble." Snot is running down her upper lip. She swipes at it and continues, "You know how I watch every cooking show on the planet?" Nicki and I nod. "Well, I tried this Rachael Ray recipe for chocolate mango scones. They were yummy. My brother had the basketball team here, and those boys ate every one. Chet Mullin said it was the best thing he ever tasted!" Even through her tears Ariel is still proud, thinking of those cute, hungry boys enjoying her scones.

"Anyway, I didn't have *unbleached* flour, so I used my baker's flour from Whole Foods. It's *bleached*." Ariel has always given way too much detail, but Nicki and I wait patiently. It's what best friends do.

"And I won with the recipe. It's supposed to be my original recipe, but it's actually Rachael Ray's. But I changed the flour. Only I don't think that is enough to really make it truly original. I mean, I didn't think I'd really win . . ." Ariel is bawling now, not even bothering to wipe at the slick of stuff pouring out of her of eyes and nose.

"I don't get it . . . you won what?" I ask.

"A contest. A baking contest. My recipe, I mean Rachael's recipe, is going to go into a cookbook. It was a contest Pillsbury ran. I mean *Pillsbury*. That's like a huge company. And they sent me $200! My name will be published in the cookbook with Rachael Ray's recipe. Well, but the flour was changed, but really that probably doesn't count . . ." Ariel grasps her bamboo mat on both ends and savagely rolls it. Stuff squishes out the ends.

Nicki comes around the counter. She takes the ruined sushi roll out of Ariel's hands and gives her a paper towel. Ariel blows her nose loudly. The kitchen smells like warm fish and body heat.

"The recipe has to be *original.* I signed the entry form swearing it was original. I mean, I was thinking, about the unbleached flour, that changing that makes it different, but it doesn't really. And I never won anything else, so it didn't seem like I ever would." Now Ariel is babbling.

"Do your parents know?" Nicki asks.

"No, not yet. I put the letter and the check in my locked music box when they came in the mail yesterday. My mom thought it was some recipes or junk mail or something from Pillsbury, so she didn't ask me anything about it."

"What are you going to do?" Ariel has stopped crying now, so I feel okay asking her about it.

"I don't know! I mean, maybe if I don't cash the check, they won't put it in the cookbook? Or maybe changing the flour does make it original? Maybe I should write a letter to Rachael Ray and see if she minds if I take credit for the recipe? Maybe I could say we collaborated? I mean, can I get seriously busted for this do you think? Like legally? And what if it comes out later? I'll never get into a good culinary academy with this on my record . . ."

"I think things are getting out of control. For all of us." Nicki has returned to her seat.

Ariel and I turn to her, surprised.

"You, M, with the whole James thing, and your mom, getting to be like a mole that won't go outside.

And now Ariel with this cooking contest thing. And me." We wait expectantly to hear what's wrong with Nicki's life. I assumed everything was okay with her until right now.

She doesn't say what's wrong though. Instead she blurts out, "I think we did that ritual wrong. We have to stop it." Nicki's voice is loud, forceful, and almost scary. She is usually so whispery and doesn't say more than a few words at a time. Ariel and I look at her in surprise.

One thing is for sure—I can see I won't have to convince them to dig up the objects.

Ariel takes a seat next to me, and we wait for Nicki to go on.

Forget Sushi, Nicki Has a Shocker

"You know how I never have you guys over to my house?" Nicki has squared her shoulders. She sits perfectly straight. Her cheekbones are sharp angles and her skin is like rich coffee with lots of milk. Her blue eyes look almost unreal. She is beautiful.

"Well, see, I have been hiding something. And it's not shame exactly, it's more, I don't know, like I didn't want to talk about it and have you guys feel sorry for me. For my family . . ."

"Nicki, you can trust us. We three are all in this . . . life situation . . . together. We're best friends. Tell us." I am dying to know what this secret could be. Instant flashes of TV-worthy horrors and scandals zing through my brain. Is she having sex with someone? Pregnant? Is her dad an alcoholic who beats her? Does she have a terminal illness . . . some melonlike tumor

eating her from inside? Her voice cuts off my terrible
fantasies.

"My brother. The baby? He's retarded." Nicki's voice
is low and sad.

"Oh, like Down syndrome?" I feel a tiny bit disappointed that the news isn't more scandalous, which
probably makes me a bad person.

"It's called Trisomy 21, which is basically the same
thing as Down syndrome. He's what they call severely
affected. And he's deaf and probably won't ever see
well. Something is wrong with his bowels too. But it's
his heart that's really bad."

Nicki is crying now. Not like Ariel was just a few
minutes ago. Instead of the loud, wet wailing, Nicki
softly weeps. Single, fat tears slide down her cheeks in
a slow progression. It is almost like they are waiting in
line, each shining droplet spacing itself behind the last
before jumping out and sliding down to her chin.

"Oh, Nicki, why didn't you tell us before?" Ariel
touches a fresh paper towel to the angle of Nicki's chin
to soak up all the tears collecting there. "I mean, it's so
sad . . ."

Nicki bats Ariel's hand away and sighs loudly.
"Exactly. I didn't want . . . that. That sorry-for-me
reaction. I mean, I haven't even lived here a year yet.
I know meeting you two, getting into your circle, was
like fate. I didn't want to jinx it. Being so close, so
bonded, has meant everything to me. Even in North

Fork, I never had such intense friendships. I guess I just didn't want to throw Noah into it. Yet. Well, till now. Does that make sense?"

I actually feel a little hurt that Nicki didn't trust us. But I nod and try to give her a sincere smile. "Yeah Nick, sure."

"I feel dumb now worrying about the cooking contest. I mean, compared to having a ... messed-up brother," Ariel sighs.

"You can say 'retarded,' Ariel. It's okay. And you are in big trouble with the cooking thing ..."

We all laugh. It feels good after all the tension in the last hour. There is a new feeling now. I know my friends feel it too. We are connecting to each other with a buzzing, electric energy. All our lives seem to be building into crises. It all stems from the ritual; I know it in my very innermost insides.

"We need to dig up the objects, undo the ritual, burn the poem of change." I speak quietly. I don't want the magic of the moment to be lost with careless words. "The book tells how to undo rituals and spells ..."

"I agree." Ariel nods. "I wished, like we were supposed to when we were reading the poem, to transform into a real chef by winning a contest. But look what has happened to me now. I got my wish, but in such a bad way, you know? I have to say I didn't believe *all the way* in that spell book, in the power, but now ..."

"My wish seems like it might come true, but in a terrible way too." Nicki interrupts Ariel. "I wanted my brother to go away. I meant like to one of those homes or something. Somewhere we could visit him a lot, but Mom wouldn't be so . . . burdened. And now it looks like he will. I mean, the doctors are saying his heart is worse, failing . . ." Nicki speaks softly. "We found out two days after the ritual. I didn't mean for him to *die*."

The three of us are very quiet for a minute. I finally break into the silence. "It's not life and death like Nicki's brother, but I did wish for my mom to be different and for James to notice me. Well, mom's officially agoraphobic." Nicki furrows her brow at me as the disease-like word trips off my tongue.

"I learned that word on Google a few days ago. It means someone who's afraid to leave the house, which IS different, but not the kind of different I was hoping for. And James certainly has noticed me. He's noticed I am a complete moronic idiot." It is obvious that we are all spiraling into chaos, we all know it.

Ariel says what we are all thinking, "Let's figure out what to do. We need to turn things around." She sounds brave now, excited.

"See if you can both sleep over on Friday." I can see how we can work this out. "We'll sneak out of my house and do the . . . unritual. My mom will be sacked out from a long day of Zoo Tycoon and Excedrin PM by ten o'clock."

Ariel and Nicki both chuckle at the funny, sad truth of this. They know about the date and how my mother has become progressively more zombie-like since then.

Plans are made. We all are smart girls. We think things through, create a time line, what we'll pack, how we'll find the objects. I feel a sense of excitement and relief. It feels good to be taking action, not just letting everything keep spiraling so out of control.

Tonight's the Night!

It's Friday at lunch. I will not say this week has been easy. In fact, it has sucked at the highest level something can. Clare quickly spread the word about the hilarious fact that I thought James was going to invite me to the dance. No one has said anything to my face, but I can feel looks of humor and pity. Thank god for Nicki and Ariel. They have made extra efforts to flank me protectively in the wide, echoing hallways and to keep an eagle eye out for James. Once we almost ran into each other, but Ariel saw him, thought fast, and yanked me into the bathroom just in time.

All we talk about now is undoing the ritual. We have studied the purple book intensely. We are so caught up in it. Before it seemed like a harmless, fun, slightly daring thing to dabble with. Now, after all that has happened, the way our wishes are biting back, well, we *believe.*

The three of us are sitting on the picnic bench that's missing a leg. The table has to be propped against the ugly aluminum side of one of those temporary buildings (I don't know why they call them that—the things are trailers). Even though the table leans and wobbles a lot, we like sitting here. It's a good spot, away from the main row of tables.

Ariel is opening opaque Tupperware containers in a row across the table. Lunch with a budding chef is always interesting. She unfolds a thin, plastic place mat. Nicki and I watch as she assembles tiny, open-faced sandwiches on the shiny surface. First she lays out neat squares of oversized brown crackers. Next come paper-thin tomato slices. Lastly, she uses a small plastic knife to put dabs of a soft-looking white cheese on top of the glistening tomatoes. She hands us each one cracker . . . thing.

"What's the cheese?" Nicki smells it suspiciously.

"Goat cheese. It's really good with tomatoes. Try it, Nicki!"

Nicki takes another sniff. "It smells kinda funky, Air."

"This is a *gourmet* appetizer." Ariel takes a huge bite, rolling her eyes at Nicki.

I try it. It's really tasty actually. Nicki eyes me, looking to see if I am showing any signs of retching or disgust. I give her a thumbs-up. Convinced I really do like it, she takes a bite too.

Her eyes widen in surprise for a moment. Goat

cheese, the first time you try it, will make you do that. She slowly nods her head toward Ariel, taking another bite. "M-hmm, it is good!"

Ariel sighs contentedly and begins to assemble three more.

"Do you really think your mom'll sleep through us sneaking out?" Ariel asks as she fusses with the tomato slices. She tosses some broken crackers over into the stubby grass behind the building where the seagulls pounce on it and scream at one another shrilly.

"Yeah, she will, trust me. Anyway, she wouldn't come look for us—that would require leaving the house. If she found out we were gone she'd probably just play Zoo Tycoon until we got back, then lecture us."

"I have the flashlights and the two garden shovels." Nicki sucks the pungent cheese off a tomato Ariel has handed her, makes a slurping sound, then continues, "I think those were the last things on our list."

I chime in, "Did we decide whether or not we should take the book? I mean, just in case we forget part of the process or the words or something? We can't afford to screw this up."

"We practically have it memorized. And it's so big and heavy, let's not." Ariel says.

Nicki leans forward in a gesture of secrecy. Ariel and I lean forward too. Our three heads almost touch and I catch a whiff of the bread and vanilla smell Ariel carries in her hair.

Nicki says shyly, "I wanted to tell you guys, I got my period last night too. Remember the book said 'look for signs of convergence'? Well, that means all three of us have it at the same time. Total convergence. And it's my first one." Nicki speaks in an awed voice. She is also a little embarrassed I think.

"Yeah, wow." I ponder this new fact. It feels like we're so grown up now that we all have our periods. It is still such a new, mysterious thing for us, this reproductive activity going on in our bodies. It seems like its own magic. And we are "converging" within it. It is no coincidence that our unritual and the magic cycles of our bodies are converging.

We have already seen other signs too. Many. For example, the moon will be only one day away from full tonight, and the tide will be extra low. Ariel was making chocolate chip cookies last night and one cookie came out of the oven with the exact shape of a spoon sketched in chocolate dots. She knew right then that the antique spoon at the bottom of the sandy pit by the bay was calling to her.

There are so many signs now that we look! I am about to tell about the bird that got in our house (an *Indian* Jay is what my mom called it—just like Nicki's sacred, buried doll!), but I stop midsentence.

Clare and one of her slutty friends are cutting around a corner of the temporary building. We wait for Clare to pass. Instead, she and the other tacky girl, Jill

I think, watch us for a moment. I see Clare's smirking face, and she turns and says something to her friend. They giggle, their exposed, flat stomachs curving in with humor. We ignore them. I have two best friends and an exciting, potentially life-changing night ahead of me. The Clares of the world are nothing to me!

The girls drift around the corner, their platform flip-flops thumping their heels. Their impossibly long, streaky hair is the last thing we see. I hate how cheap and beautiful they look. We resume our discussion.

"My brother's surgery is Monday, so this is just in time." Since telling us about Noah last weekend, Nicki has really opened up. The baby has to have something in his heart fixed, and it is a risky surgery. Nicki is sure he'll come through it fine, thanks to tonight's ceremony. She even says we can come over to her house and meet him, finally, when he gets back home.

"It's really just in time for us all, doing this tonight. I feel like we all need things to change, but maybe change back." As I speak I picture my weirdly empty house. Empty, even with Mom in it. I think of how I don't seem to exist at school or at home, only when I am with Nicki and Ariel. Tonight will change that.

"And this whole mess with the cooking contest will get sorted out too!" Ariel sounds slightly shrill and very desperate.

The bell rings. Nicki and I help Ariel pack up all her little containers. The wind picks up suddenly and brings faint sounds from the bay—low, echoing blasts of freighters sounding their horns, a muffled voice announcing a ferry, perhaps, and seagulls. Always seagulls. The timing of the unexpected wind seems fated, another cosmic form of communication with us. Everything is an omen.

We have two more classes to get through. Tonight is the night. Tonight we will fix things so that our lives quit throwing us off center every time we turn around.

Preparing

We decide to walk the Bay Farm Island trail after school, in the daylight, and mark the hole's location. Even with the almost-full moon tonight, it might be hard to find the spot where we buried the stuff. Nicki, smartly, thought of this possibility when she saw the weather on the news this morning.

It is supposed to get foggy. We know from our years in Alameda what could happen: a thick, wet fog creeping from the Pacific Ocean toward our bay. Full moons and shining stars are no match for this type of cottonlike San Francisco fog. We will need to mark the spot today and bring flashlights tonight. We will leave nothing to chance.

School's finally over. We are walking at a fast pace, single file, toward the bridge. We have to wait on the main island side of the footbridge because, just as we round the corner, the bridge begins to split and lift. An enormous sailboat waits patiently to pass through.

We stand to the side and wait, watching. No matter how many times we have all seen the bridges break themselves in two, it is still kind of awesome. Finally the boat can pass. It glides slowly, its motor barely makes a sound. The jumble of rolled materials, ropes, pulleys, and poles looks complicated, and I marvel that anyone can learn to sail when confronted with such a mess of equipment.

"You know," Ariel says thoughtfully, almost as though she is speaking to herself, not to us. "I have lived in Alameda all my life and I have never been on a sailboat."

"Me neither. Just the ferries from here and Jack London Square," I admit.

"I've been sailing a bunch of times." We turn to Nicki in surprise.

"But you haven't even lived here a year yet . . ." Ariel sounds mad, which makes no sense. Who cares if Nicki has been sailing?

"Not here, no." Nicki shakes her head. "In Southern California. Catalina? My mom's uncle has a sailboat. We visited whenever my dad had to go to L.A. . . ."

"So you're already a sailor, huh?" Ariel sounds playful and smiles at Nicki. I think she knows she seemed hostile before and is self-correcting. I do that too sometimes— say or act a certain way without really meaning to.

"It was when I was little, but I do remember it. I remember ducking all the time . . ."

Nicki trails off, and we watch in silence. The two halves of the bridge sticking up in the air look like giant Lego towers. Finally the sailboat is clear and the main bridge to Bay Farm Island begins to lower. Lines of cars restart their engines. They inch forward by tiny bits in impatience, waiting for the bridge to become whole again.

I have a sudden yearning to sail, and I say, "Let's all agree, right now, to go sailing together. You know, someday." I picture the three of us manning a glossy craft with pluming white sails. Ariel will make little finger sandwiches and cold lemonade. We will wear sun visors and our shoes will be blinding white. We will not wear socks.

"I hereby promise to go sailing with my two best friends someday!" Ariel makes a cross over her chest with her index finger.

"Absolutely!" Nicki imitates her gesture.

It has to happen. "Cool," I say.

We walk along quietly for awhile. Ariel's red head bobs in front of me and Nicki's thwacking flip-flops follow behind. We are well onto the curve of the trail in no time, our pace is so fast.

We have been walking about ten minutes. It is one of those days that is so impossibly clear, it's like everything has extra edges. Even the sky seems to be defined by angles. San Francisco looks unreal somehow, like an artist's image of itself. We are all quiet, enjoying this moment, this day, this sense of connection and anticipation.

Ariel stops suddenly, and I almost run into her.

"What?" Nicki tilts her head in question as she too stops quickly in the middle of the path.

"I think we're getting close. To where we buried our stuff. Remember, it was by that mucky, wet area? And remember the tree with the grayish leaves and a crooked trunk?" Ariel swings her head back and forth. She points to a crooked tree just above the path and sweeps her arm in an arc to point at a boggy spot. Bright orange California poppies ring a damp depression halfway between the path and the water's edge.

I search my own memory, examine the tree. This is all wrong. "No, it's farther up. That tree's crookedness isn't right. And I remember thinking it was a straight line to Coit Tower when I looked up . . ."

We all look across the bay. The unmistakable cylinder of Coit Tower is still to the left of us, not straight ahead.

"I think M is right," Nicki says.

"Okay." Ariel sounds doubtful.

We continue walking. I spot the tree. I remember the way its crooked trunk looked like an upside-down water faucet. I stop and again find Coit Tower in my line of vision. Yep, we are exactly across from it.

"It's here. This is the place." Nicki and Ariel look all around, searching their own memories for clues to confirm the location. We all look at the ground, but there is no sign of the hole. But there wouldn't be; it's been months now.

Ariel shakes her head. "I don't know, M, it doesn't seem right . . ."

Nicki remains silent.

"I remember the tree, exactly THAT tree. True, the mucky area isn't here, but it had been raining then and hasn't in awhile, so that would explain it. It dried up. And Coit . . . look." I stick my arms out and turn my wrists up, thumbs pointing to each other, and create a three-sided finger frame. Coit's beige cylinder is framed neatly in the middle. "We're exactly across, just like I remember."

Ariel crosses her arms beneath her chest and makes rainbow shapes in the silty dirt with her shoe. "I just think maybe it was a *different* crooked tree . . ."

Ariel's resistance to my certainty seems to make me feel more confident and certain somehow. In fact, I am so positive we have found the right place, I want to scream at her. Instead I take a breath, turn to Nicki.

She looks from Ariel to me and shrugs before looking down. Her hair hides her expression, but I already know it. She is unsure. She doesn't want to take a side. Nicki lacks a spine sometimes.

She sighs, knowing her opinion must go against

one of us and that she must express it to break the tie. "Look, I don't have a photographic memory, so I don't know. I mean, we didn't plan on having to find it again, we didn't know we'd need to dig everything back up . . . anyway, if you're so sure, M, well I believe you." She looks at Ariel, not me, as she speaks. I hear Ariel huff out a breath of frustration.

"The only way we are going to know for sure is when we actually dig, right? And we can't, I mean until tonight, when we are actually *doing* the ceremony . . ."

"Nicki's right." Ariel gives me a tight smile. We are narrowly escaping a fight, and we both know it.

"Look, guys," Nicki, the peacemaker, continues, "we have a whole roll of tape so let's mark this tree AND any other place Ariel might think is right. Like that one place farther back on the trail. Tonight, if we can't find the stuff in one spot, we'll try another . . ."

"All right, okay." It is too reasonable and logical for me to argue with, but I am sure that marking anywhere else will be a waste of time.

It takes us another hour to finish the loop of the trail. We mark three spaces with the reflective tape. The elation and excitement of earlier are gone. Now we seem to be walking with a sense of dread. The day's crispness is becoming blurred and ruined with a damp air blowing in. The fog is already on the move; we can see the thick gray mass, like a solid wall, enfolding the red arches of the Golden Gate Bridge.

We have not talked much to each other since disagreeing about the spot. Ariel sighs loudly, giving voice to my own feelings of frustration. She stops and sits down in the middle of the trail: Nicki and I lower ourselves on each side of her. She grabs our hands and squeezes. "If we have the right spot, let us receive a sign." The three of us stare intently out across the rippled water. We all send out a silent wish for a sign.

We are going to Ariel's house before going back to mine so we can pick up her overnight bag. We had to pass her house after school anyway, so Nicki left her stuff at Ariel's too. We'll grab their bags and head to my house for dinner and "sleeping" over. My mom is going to splurge and let us walk to get takeout from Kiri, the best Japanese restaurant on the planet.

We are busy planning what we'll eat. Ariel is arguing against tempura and Nicki is refusing to eat any more sushi. We are so lost in conversation that we fail to notice several cars double-parked next to Ariel's house. It isn't until we are right in front of Mrs. Rosencrantz's house that we become aware of anything outside of ourselves.

Mrs. Rosencrantz's front door stands open. Three old ladies huddle on the front porch. We scoot past, perplexed. Ariel's brother greets us at the door.

Before we can ask, he says, "Mrs. Rosencrantz died!" His tone is almost gleeful; I think he enjoys being able to tell us such dramatic news, hopes to shock us.

"Oh my god." Ariel gasps and claps her hand to her mouth. She turns to looks at Nicki and me in disbelief, then her cheeks instantly bloom with color that almost matches her hair. "This is the sign. A terrible sign . . ."

Her brother snorts at her, shakes his head, and heads past us out the door.

We follow Ariel to her room.

Anything Can Be a Sign, Right?

"I can't believe it. I just saw her, got cornered by her, a few days ago!" Ariel is crying a little. Nicki and I sit on her bed and watch her pace.

"It's creepy." Nicki says in agreement.

Ariel uses a bandana from the floor to dab at her eyes, sits on her bed. "I mean, I am not really sad sad about it, but I feel weird. I never knew anyone who died before. And we always said such mean stuff about her!"

Ariel's mom peeks around the doorway, and gives a little knock of announcement. "Hi, girls. I guess you know about Mrs. Rosencrantz."

We all nod.

"It *is* very sad, but she was old and she had a good life, girls. Don't be too upset. Have your sleepover tonight and try not to think about poor Mrs. Rosencrantz."

Ariel's mom is one of those types that is always

cheerful, even sometimes when it doesn't seem exactly appropriate. When we were in second grade, Ariel's cat got hit by a car. Her mom told Ariel he was in Kitty Heaven now, and then cheerfully offered us cookies. I remember this incident as she talks to us about Mrs. Rosencrantz. She will not allow us to mope around about this.

"What happened to her, Mom?"

"Apparently a stroke. Her church friends came to check on her today when she didn't show up for her volunteer shift at the Bargain Basket. Anyway, it looks like it was fast, painless."

Ariel's mom sits on the bed, scooting Nicki over a bit, and slaps her palms down on her legs to break the bleak mood. "I think you girls should go on and enjoy your evening now!"

"It's just so, so . . . unbelievable, Mom." Ariel has stopped crying now. Her voice sounds almost normal. "We just *saw* her."

"Yes, well," she nods, shrugs. "What do you girls have planned for tonight?"

I can feel all three of us invisibly freeze up a little at this question. I answer quickly, "Oh the usual. Nothing special."

Nicki and Ariel mutter in overly bored agreement.

"Okay, well don't stay up too late. Ariel, be home by lunch tomorrow. We have to run out to Berkeley in the afternoon, and you can swing by the Berkeley Bowl if you want." The Berkeley Bowl is a chef's paradise of gourmet, unpronounceable foods.

"Cool, Mom. I'll be home by then."

"I know death is hard to wrap your head around girls, at your age. Even at my age actually." She looks at each of us in turn with a mother-understands sort of look. "But try and let this one go for now, okay?" She kisses Ariel on the head and leaves, closing the door behind her.

"I feel weird. About Mrs. Rosencrantz. We were asking for a sign, and I think this is a sign . . . that we *shouldn't* do the ceremony tonight after all." Nicki speaks in a hushed voice tinged with worry. "I am Indian, and I think I am really tuned in to this stuff."

Ariel picks up a raggedy *Bon Appétit* magazine from her floor and fans the pages in little arcs as she speaks. "It's not a sign, Nicki, I mean, I thought it was, but now I think how could it be? Mrs. Rosencrantz, her dying, is so not related to us . . . and you're only half Indian, right? I think it's a total coincidence that Mrs. Rosencrantz died today. Nothing more."

"I think Ariel's right." I don't personally know if this is a sign or not, but I feel certain we shouldn't blow this chance to go get those things dug up. It's planned, our night is cleared, and we've marked the spot . . . spots. We can't wait! Nicki's brother's surgery is in three days, my mom is getting stranger as we speak, my social life lives somewhere in the toilet, and Ariel's cooking contest problem could be discovered any moment. No, we can't afford to miss our chance tonight.

Nicki sighs. "Okay, but if anything else happens . . . well, I just have a feeling we shouldn't do this. I mean, maybe not right now, tonight."

Ariel tosses the magazine aside in a gesture of irritation. "Look Nicki, we can make anything we want be a sign. Doesn't mean it's really a sign, you know? Like I could say, that cloud looks like a fish, must be a sign, or hey, I found a penny from the year I was born, must be a sign . . ."

"Fine, Ariel!" Nicki interrupts. "Okay, I get it. Let's just go then."

"Things'll work out tonight, and *zen our probleems vil joos melt avay*," I say in a corny, fortune-teller voice. It works, and they both burst out laughing.

The short walk to my house is pleasant. We discuss our potential crushes (I am encouraged to forget James but I've still got it for him, unfortunately), we agree that Nicki is sooo lucky to have long black lashes *without* mascara, and all three of us decide to try and give up dairy for a week to see if it really does help our skin. Ariel feels that butter should be excluded from the diet though, because she can't cook anything without at least butter, so we agree butter won't count.

As we come up my street I see Aunt Winda's car parked in front of our house. I didn't know she had planned to visit. We clatter up our red painted steps and I fling the door open hard, the way Mom hates.

Aunt Winda is sitting on the sofa. She gives us a big, cheery smile. "Hi, girls! I know you're too old for a babysitter, so let's say I am your . . . older companion tonight!"

I am confused. "Where's Mom?"

"She's at an appointment. We'll talk about it later, Miss M. She's fine, good, just out." Aunt Winda gives me a look that says I should not push for information right now. I am shocked that my mother is *anywhere* out of the house.

"Now you girls just do whatever you do. I'm around. Oh, and I'll be staying tonight too."

My heart sinks. Staying? Aunt Winda is both a night owl AND a light sleeper. Great, how will we sneak out now? There is no avoiding *this* sign—it is slapping us in the face. Mutely, Ariel and Nicki follow me to my room.

To Go or Not to Go

There are squeaky, hinged Styrofoam containers and little lidded cups all over the floor in my room. Aunt Winda said to get whatever we wanted, on her credit card, and so we did. We ordered way too much food, but it's Moshi. I mean, serious yum factor. We are all sitting on my bed trying to balance our plates. Every time one of us needs something else—more rice or some ginger—we have to get up and kneel on the floor. It is not an ideal way to eat a meal, but we wanted privacy.

When we got home from getting the food, Aunt Winda asked me to come in the kitchen alone. She said she wanted to make herself a plate before we picked over everything. Ariel and Nicki caught her tone, knew she wanted to talk to me alone, and quickly walked down the long corridor to my room.

Aunt Winda peeked in each container. She used a

fork to made careful piles of chicken teriyaki, rice, and California rolls on a paper plate. As she fussed with dipping sauces and wasabi, she told me that my mother was seeing a therapist in the city.

She tried to sound matter-of-fact, casual, unworried, but I could tell she had the jitters as she spoke. Aunt Winda told me she had found a doctor for my mother to see a month ago. This Dr. Stanfield person specializes in anxiety disorders, specifically agoraphobics (she was surprised I knew the word, but *duh,* I live with one). She told me my mother had had two previous appointments scheduled for when I was in school, but she hadn't been able to get herself out of the house to go. I giggled inappropriately when Aunt Winda told me this . . . I mean, wouldn't that be an obvious problem?

Anyway, this doctor had a last-minute cancellation and had called my mom to see if she could come into the city and take the appointment. Aunt Winda happened to be here when this doctor called. My mom didn't want to go, using me and the sleepover as an excuse, but Aunt Winda wouldn't let her out of it. She said she'd drive mom into the city AND be back to stay with us for the sleepover. She wouldn't allow Mom not to go. I could see it happening—my aunt is so overbearing sometimes.

I asked, at that point in the story, why Mom wouldn't just come home. I mean, how long does it take to see a mental doctor—like an hour or two?

Aunt Winda then told me that Mom was such a wreck before leaving that she had taken some "calming medication." I said, "Oh, you drugged her," and Aunt Winda gave me a look. I shut up.

Mom is going to stay in Aunt Winda's apartment tonight, alone, presumably with more "calming medication." We're picking her up in the morning. Wow. I mean, holy crap.

I could tell, as my Aunt rambled on and picked at her chicken, that she and my mom have talked a lot about her staying-home-being-depressed thing. Aunt Winda said Mom knew and worried (mostly for me) that she was sinking, getting steadily worse.

At that point I had heard enough. I felt betrayed and excluded to know they had been talking about it and no one asked me or told me anything. I mean, she's my mother, this is my house. I could have told Aunt Winda all about how she's gotten worse since the date disaster. I have been sick with worry, messing with magic, for god's sake, hoping to pull her out of it. And I could have gone with her to that doctor.

I wanted to tell her that I had something secret and powerful, something I know will help mom, but I didn't want my aunt to know about the book. I feel certain the book wants me to guard it, and in turn it will allow me to use its secrets to help my mom. To help me too. Aunt Winda was still talking, but I was thinking about the book, blocking her out.

Whatever. I was done with this conversation so I didn't say anything. The book would ultimately solve it all. I just wanted to go eat mounds of Japanese food and giggle with my friends. I said something inappropriate like "groovy!" and my aunt finally stopped talking.

I grabbed the wobbly stack of containers, balancing them against my body, and stormed out. Aunt Winda just dipped sushi in soy sauce and watched me go. Some sticky sauce leaked out of the tilted food boxes, dampening my shirt and puddling near the bottom of my (sadly, nearly empty) bra as I tried to balance everything. It would have made more sense to make two trips to get the food, but I didn't want to have to see my aunt again. I didn't want to think about Mom right now.

Hearing Aunt Winda talk about "meds" and "anxiety" and "chronic" this and that made me feel angry. Furious in fact. It hit me halfway down the hall. I had told my aunt "I got it," but I didn't really. I know I sounded smart mouthed and uncaring too. All these things zipped through my mind. I pushed open my door and my friends scrambled up to help me with the tower of food. Ariel and Nicki were a welcome sight right then.

Now we are in my room, stuffing ourselves. Eating the flaky salmon and crispy tempura is bringing me this exquisite feeling of comfort. It's like the food is my own "calming medication." I tell me friends about my mom between bites.

Nicki feels like it is another sign that we shouldn't go out tonight and try to redirect the magic. She thinks that my mom getting help is proof that things are already turning around on their own. She thinks Mom being gone is a sign that we should stay. Ariel disagrees.

I sit back and just listen to them argue. My pig collection stares back at me from behind Nicki, all these beady eyes buried in mounds of flesh. They seem like unwanted intruders now more than ever.

I feel strange. It all washes over me as my stomach heaves a little, overfull. I mean, all in one day we found out Mrs. Rosencrantz died and that my mom is a serious head case. We're having our first real fight, and tonight's THE night. It is overwhelming. I feel a new level of sureness about the power the rituals can have. They must feel it too.

I also have a sense of urgency and foreshadowing, as if the events of the day might not compare to what the night will bring.

Nicki and Ariel argue on . . .

The Splitting of Friends

"Nicki, you're doing it again"—Ariel points a chopstick at Nicki—"seeing signs everywhere."

Nicki slowly cracks her knuckles. She is looking down as she speaks. "I am tired of you running the show, Ariel. *You* don't know anymore about what is a sign than we do. And I think this is a sign. Signs aren't necessarily hocus-pocus magic things you know. Sometimes it's just *common sense* to look around and see what's logical. Besides, M said her aunt will probably stay awake late, so we can't slip out anyway. Don't you see, there are signs—no, *realities*—all over the place telling us this *isn't* going to work tonight!"

I have never seen Nicki so fired up. Her face is blooming with heat and color as she stands up and crosses her arms, waiting for Ariel to deny it. My pig collection stands silently at her back. They look like they're waiting to see what she'll do too.

I can't stand having them fight. This night is getting ruined before it's even started. "Guys, come on, don't yell at each other."

"I have just been thinking a lot about it." Nicki sits back down. She doesn't sound mad anymore, just sad. "I really do think there are forces and powers around us, call it magic or whatever. I think we started something back when we did the ritual. I think that poem we found is so . . . true. I think we did create, I don't know, momentum, that's changing our lives. Or maybe we just *think* we did. Maybe it doesn't make any difference because either way, things are happening. Maybe we didn't know what we were doing. Maybe we should just . . . stop. Maybe it's all just us *wishing* it were real, and it's not. Maybe that's how the book works."

This is the longest speech I have ever heard Nicki make. And it is hard to follow. I am not exactly sure what she is saying. Too many maybe's.

Ariel is making little green wasabi flowers with her chopsticks. She sighs. "Whatever Nicki. It's sad you are so, so . . . unable to imagine that this stuff IS real, I mean look at our lives right now—"

"No, not 'whatever Nicki,'" Nicki angrily interrupts. She stands up, brushes her lap and flicks her hair back. She turns away from us and eyeballs a pig with silver wings and a wire halo. She tweaks the halo a bit before turning back to us. "I am going home. I don't want to do this. I am going to play with my brother. I don't have much time left to see him before the surgery."

Ariel jumps to her feet, "Nicki, no! Wait, I'm sorry! Come on, don't be like this! How can you not do this, at least try, for your brother . . ."

I interrupt, join in the begging. "Please Nicki, I feel like we need to do the ceremony tonight. I *feel* it, don't leave." I try to sound both convincing and pathetic.

Nicki is stuffing her sweatshirt into her bag, not looking at us. "You two do whatever you want, count me out. I *feel* like it's probably just useless anyway, three girls playing with supposed magic? Looking for signs? My brother might die, M's mom is whacked, and Ariel's practically a criminal." (I hear Ariel huff out a little sound of anger at this last comment.) "Digging up our buried trinkets won't change it, any of it! Don't you see, everything's just, just . . . going to hell? Spells from a sidewalk sale book and three seventh graders can't fix all this."

She slams out my door. Ariel and I sit in silence. We are stunned. Who knew Nicki could be so forceful? So pissed? Wow. She has betrayed us.

This is terrible. I feel panicked. We *have to do this thing tonight,* turn things around. I think of the present moment: One of my best friends has just stormed out in anger. The other is fuming and silent. My screwed-up mother is popping pills in my aunt's house. School life is in even worse condition; I spend all day trying to be invisible and avoiding Clare and her friends or James and his.

I think of Nicki's brother. He needs all the help he can get, and his own sister won't even try and give it to him. And there's Ariel. She's committed perjury or forgery (or is it plagiarism?), not to mention the way it could kill her dream of becoming a chef. All this whirls through my mind in seconds.

I stare at the purple book, open to the undoing ritual we plan to perform. I am not about to let tonight, this opportunity, slip through my fingers. I take the poem of change out, where we had stashed it for tonight (we have to burn it and bury its ashes in the hole once we have retrieved our three things). I smooth it across my knees.

"We have to go without her."

Ariel stares at me for a long time. I feel like something is tilting, like Ariel is moving away from me somehow. Her eyes slide away, and I can tell I won't like to hear what she has to say.

"No, M, maybe Nicki's right." She looks down at the floor, her shoulders rounded and her hands fisted into a lump. There is something raw and almost childish about her tone, as though her voice is naked. "It's just, well, I want to believe in all this, and I really did, for a while. Maybe I still do, but just now, when I heard what Nicki was saying . . ."—she comes and sits by me on the bed—"I think she kind of made sense. I saw us how she was saying. It's stupid really . . . looking for signs, burying dumb toys, thinking this witchcrafty stuff is real."

"Ariel, it IS!" I can't believe she's saying this. "The book, I mean you read it too! These spells, this kind of magic is super old, the Indians and ancient man believed—"

Ariel interrupts me. "M . . . it's, I don't know, it's ruined now, you know? I am going to go home too. I think I need to tell my parents what I've done. Maybe write a letter to Rachael Ray or something. I have to figure out what to do, how to clean up my mess. I need to do something *real*." She is nesting the food containers neatly as she speaks. "Sneaking out to the bay and trying to find that hole and dig up the stuff we buried isn't going to fix anything."

"Ariel, maybe it will! I mean, isn't it worth a try? Don't leave too! How can you just give up? How can we know it won't work?"

She slings her knapsack over her shoulder. She's crying a little. "I'll call you tomorrow."

I have too much pride to follow her. I hear the front door close a few seconds later, Aunt Winda calling good-bye. Then her footsteps come toward me down the hall and she is sticking her head in my room.

"I thought your friends were sleeping over?"

I give her a look that warns her I don't want to talk about it. "No."

She catches on, nods her head, and scoots away. I close my door and collapse on my bed. I have no idea what to do with myself.

After a short while the phone rings and I hear my aunt answer. A minute later she's knocking on my door again.

"Telephone, Ms. M." She opens the door only wide enough to stick her hand through and thrust the phone toward me. "Do you want it?"

I figure it's Nicki or Ariel calling to make up. "Sure, thanks." I smile at Aunt Winda and hold out my hand. She comes in, ruffles my hair, winks, and hands me the phone. Yep, must be one of them.

"Hey," I say, settling back onto my bed, getting ready for a long chat about our silly fight.

The person on the other end coughs uncomfortably. It takes me a second to recognize that cough. It's my dad.

"Hi, honey, it's Dad." He still seems to be working something out of his throat, or maybe he's nervous.

"Oh. Dad. Hi." I know I sound disappointed, but I can't help it.

"So how are you?"

"Fine."

Uncomfortable silence. More throat clearing.

"Well, okay Matilda. Fine, that's great. I called to say hello to you but also to see how you feel about your mom. I mean about what your mom's going through with the . . . the problems . . ."

I cut him off. "She's working stuff out, and Aunt Winda's here. It's not like I'm not safe or something, Dad."

He sighs. I picture him tapping his foot like he always does when he gets worked up. "I talked to your mother, and your aunt too earlier today, and we all thought you should have the option of maybe coming here for awhile. You know, with me . . ."

I literally snort when he says this. "I live here dad. In Alameda. I don't want to move. My friends are here. My life is here!"

"I know, I know," he rushes on, "but your mother thinks it's a little rough for you now. She worries about you, Matilda, and she wanted to give you the choice."

"I choose staying here, in my home. No offense, Dad. Mom is kinda messed up, but she's trying to get better. She will too. And it's not like her playing Zoo Tycoon all day and not taking me to the mall is *abusive* . . ."

"No one is saying that." Dad doesn't sound so nervous now, more just tired. I think he's probably relieved I don't want to live with him. I flash on a picture of his small apartment, scarcely decorated and without color. No, it wouldn't work, not on any level.

"Thanks for the offer though." I feel a tiny bit bad for him too at this point.

"If you change your mind or just want to talk, I am here. I love you. I'll try and call more too, okay?" I have to admit he sounds sincere. He sounds like he is truly concerned for me, and it makes me unexpectedly sad.

"Okay, Dad. But it'll all be okay. I mean with Mom and all."

"Well all right then, I'll let you go. It sounds like you have something to do."

I realize he's right. I an overwhelmed with feelings . . . about my friends, the book, my mom, my dad . . . I am going to cry. I have to hang up before he catches on.

We say good bye quickly. I crawl under my quilt and let the musty, familiar cotton settle over my face before the first tears leak out.

One Is a Lonesome Number

I cry for a long time. Aunt Winda must hear me, but
she doesn't come back to check on me. I think about my
mom being gone, and realize it feels no different than
normal life. What feels terrible is the absence of Nicki
and Ariel. Not their physical absence, but the fact that I
can't call them now. This kind of alone is scary.

I could talk to Aunt Winda I guess, but what can she
do? Besides, she is so worried about Mom I don't think
she needs or wants to hear about the mess of my life. I
think of calling Dad back. I try to summon up the way
he made me feel so protected when I was very small.
He used to bring me little presents, pig things usually,
when I hit rough patches. Obviously it has been way
too long since he comforted me about anything. This
last phone call lasted about five minutes, and he barely
asked me about anything. If I called back now, I feel

certain he'd just get off the phone quickly and send me some sort of pig the next day. Of course, he'd use overnight FedEx to show he really cares. No, Dad's out.

When I finally stop crying I am very calm. I feel like a picture in a museum. I am hollow, cleansed. I look in the mirror. I look tragic. My cheeks flame bright pink and my eyes look incredibly blue against the bright red background. My long cry has produced eyelids that puff plumply. I think the half-lidded look they give me is kind of sexy. My hair is tousled and slightly ratty. If James saw me now *he* would want to comfort me.

I carefully pack my backpack with a flashlight, the hand shovel I took from our cobwebby back shed earlier today, a matchbook pinched from Moshi just tonight, the book with the poem tucked inside, and a bottle of water. Strangely, as I prepare to go, I am thinking of Mrs. Rosencrantz.

I can't picture her dead. In fact, I can't even absorb the *fact* of her death. I haven't known anyone who's died. It seems somehow impossible, as though someone being alive one minute and then just gone the next is like a cool illusion, no more believable.

Now I must get past Aunt Winda. I haven't planned how yet. I go into the hall and place my backpack gently on the floor beside my door. I can hear the muted sound of the TV. I stroll into the living room. Aunt Winda is flipping through channels. A large glass of urine-colored wine and a bag of Doritos are on the table in front of her.

She looks up at me as I come in. I see her eyes register my tragic face, but she says nothing. She grabs the chips instead and holds them out to me. I take a few, plop down beside her. I am suddenly hungry, as though the crying jag has burned up all the food I ate not an hour ago.

"Tough night, kiddo?" She continues to channel flip as she asks. She doesn't look at me. Sometimes it seems like adults have all had the same class on how to handle kids with a problem. I've seen teachers, parents, coaches, etc., all use the don't-push-the-young-person-to-talk-but-give-them-an-opening-to-talk-and-sound-casual-and-avoid-direct-eye-contact technique Aunt Winda is using now. I am supposed to think she is only vaguely interested in why my friends stormed out and why my face looks like it's been sandpapered. I am supposed to feel safe and comfortable expressing myself. I play along.

"We are all in a huge fight." I grab some more chips, crunch them slowly.

She takes a slug of her wine, still doesn't look at me, but stops channel flipping. She's landed on a home shopping channel. A lady is grinding up vegetables in an oddly shaped contraption. It looks like a short, fat vacuum cleaner hose attached to a funnel. Sludgy stuff oozes out the tubed end and the lady catches it in little paper cups. The audience reaches eagerly for the Dixie cups of nasty goop, wearing ridiculous looks of pure pleasure as they choke it down.

Aunt Winda shifts beside me so she can touch my knee. "I know this day, with your mom going like she has, and this . . . falling out with your friends, probably isn't ranking as one of your better days, M."

I can feel her waiting for me to agree and emote. I do agree, but I've already cried out all my tears; I feel focused now, not upset. I am focused on getting out to the bay.

"Aunt Winda, I need to go over to Ariel's, talk to her about some stuff . . ."

"It's late hon, almost nine, maybe tomorrow? Or you could call her on the phone?"

"I don't want to go into it all right now,"—I shake my head, try to seem completely pathetic—"but I really need to talk to her in person. And it's only a few blocks, there're streetlights, and I've gone over there this late before."

I can feel Aunt Winda wavering about what to do. Normally she would offer to drive me, but she would never drive when she's had alcohol. And I know my mom would probably say no, I have never walked over to Ariel's alone at night, but Aunt Winda doesn't know that either.

"Please, Aunt Winda, I need to do this. And I can call you when I get there and Ariel's brother can walk me back . . . he's in high school." I make eye contact with her as I speak and then fall into what I hope is dejected and pitiful silence.

The lady on television is cramming whole stalks of celery and some potatolike globs into the mouth of her machine. Now the sludge looks like cat throw-up. Aunt Winda is sucking Dorito cheese off her fingers, daintily, one by one, and trying to decide if she should let me go.

"Okay, Miss M, go."

I sigh, say in a small voice, "Don't worry Aunt Winda, no big deal here. I just can't fight with Ariel like this and sleep tonight . . . so, anyway, thanks."

"Call me when you get there, and if her brother can't walk you home call me again and I'll come for you."

"It takes like five minutes to walk there Aunt Winda, but I guess if you want, I'll call you." I don't have a cell so I'll have to find a pay phone.

"And don't be out too late. Do you have a curfew?"

"Not really, but I'll be back by, say, midnight?"

"Isn't that late for a seventh grader?"

"Yeah, maybe sort of, but this is a . . . special circumstance, I think."

Aunt Winda gives up, sighs, drains the last of her wine. "I trust you, Miss M. And I know your mom does. Go on then, go make up with Ariel." She resumes channel flipping. Thank god, that infomercial was really grossing me out.

I go get my backpack. I kiss Aunt Winda on the cheek and reassure her I will not be kidnapped or otherwise waylaid on my three-block, well-lit journey.

I feel guilty about lying, but I have no choice. I am on my way.

Silly Me, I Thought Things Couldn't Get More Bizarre

As soon as I round the corner to Park Street, I begin to run. My backpack bangs painfully into my lower back. A dog barks suddenly to my left, and I sprint past. I plan to find a pay phone in town. I will call Aunt Winda and say I'm at Ariel's. I am crossing my fingers Aunt Winda won't try and call Ariel before I get to a phone. I don't think she would unless I wait too long to call. I have begged my Mom for a cell phone for months, and now I wish I had worked her harder.

My lungs are starting to burn a little. There is a frigid wind blowing in sharp, quick bursts, and it pushes against me, as if trying to force me backward. I am running on the sidewalk in the main part of downtown Alameda now, and there are many people out and about. It is a Friday, and the restaurants are full.

Many of the secondhand and consignment stores that line Park Street are still open. I hope I don't see anyone I know. I hope it looks like I am jogging, not running in a half-panic like I really am. The backpack isn't helping my cover though.

I spot a pay phone at the gas station on Park and Encinal. Yes! I've only been running about five minutes. I swing my backpack to the ground and take long, deep breaths. My heart is knocking into my chest and my right side has a pinching cramp just beneath my rib cage. Traffic whooshes by as the light at the intersection turns green. I'll wait until it's red again before I call. Aunt Winda might notice traffic noises and get suspicious.

I wait another minute before calling. I am breathing more or less normally now. I feel warm, electric. Okay, dial. Wait! I didn't think to bring change for the phone! No! I shake my backpack hopefully. A few quarters clink in the side pocket. The signs are coming thick and fast. I mean, first I get out right under my aunt's nose, and now, as if by magic, quarters I forgot I'd need for the pay phone have appeared. I wish Ariel and Nicki could see me now.

Aunt Winda answers on the second ring. "Hi, Miss M, I guess you got there?"

A car with a loud stereo goes by and I wince. "Yep, just got here." I am lying so well, so easily, I am amazed. I never knew I had this skill.

"Can her brother walk you home?"

"Oh, yeah, uh-huh. Don't worry, and you don't have to wait up . . ."

"I'll be up. Midnight, right? Oh, and your mom called, said she'd talk all this out with you tomorrow, when she gets home. She said good night."

"Okay. Well, see you in a bit!" I try to sound cheery but in a hurry to get off the phone. The unavoidable noises of a gas station pay phone put me at risk every second.

"I hope you guys work thinks out, M." Her voice is so soft and caring. I feel momentarily guilty.

"Thanks, I think we will. Okay, bye!"

"Bye hon."

I shoulder my pack and start walking up Park. Families with tired children drag out of restaurants and groups of teenagers huddle on corners, smoking cigarettes. I pass El Sombrero and purposely don't look inside its cheery windows.

No one seems to notice me, alone, a bit too young for this time of evening. I get to the corner by the mall and I can see the faint glimmer of the water straight ahead. The dank, egglike smell the bay sometimes gets fills my nostrils. It will take me about five minutes more to get to the paved frontage trail which spans the Alameda beach. I can follow the path all the way up and over to Bay Farm Island. I am lost in thought as I walk. I feel brave and determined.

I repeat the lines I will say when I find the trinkets. The rune of undoing. The spell of reversal. The unritual. I have it well memorized. I feel utterly certain that it will truly work a change, or maybe a changing back, in my life and in the lives of my two friends. Even though they aren't here, and we're technically in a fight, this whole thing is still about all three of us.

I can already picture Ariel and Nicki when I tell them about sneaking out to the lonely dirt trail and courageously digging and chanting alone. They won't be able to apologize enough for making the mistake of abandoning me to do this by myself. They will shake their heads at my foolish bravery. I'll accept their apologies and try not to look smug.

I will see awe in Nicki's eyes as I recount digging up the trinkets. My fingers will be bandaged, the cuticles puffed and jagged from my work. She'll cry a little as she talks about the miraculous recovery her brother is making. She'll polish the grit from the Indian mother's eyes and resew the papoose's little, rotting jacket.

Ariel will hug me and shake her head in wonder. She'll be holding a letter from Rachael Ray saying it's fine to take credit for the recipe. Rachael will be awed by Ariel's honesty and talent, and promise to recommend her to the Culinary Institute personally.

My mother will come home cured, almost miraculously, tomorrow. She'll shake her head in wonder at the last few months, sheepishly talk about her staying home too much, and how that one appointment just snapped her out of it all somehow. We'll go out shopping after school at least once a week. She'll suggest small weekend trips to Napa, Big Sur, and Santa Cruz. She'll have a date every Saturday we manage to stay home. She'll resell her Tycoon games on eBay.

I am so absorbed in these conjured images that I fail to notice at first that someone is calling my name.

"Mattie, hey Mattie!"

I stop walking. Two men in spandex shorts whiz by me on in-line skates. A young couple pushing a stroller and speaking Spanish pass my other side. It feels like time has become thick and slow as I stand there stupidly.

It's James who has called me. Yes, James. Here. Now. He's with two of his friends and they each hold a skateboard. They are punching each other's shoulders and laughing as they approach me. Can I be swallowed now by the earth, please?

I Don't Get Where I Meant to Go, but I End Up in a Good Place

I hate that James looks so beautiful walking over here. I still hate him for witnessing my humiliation. I hate him for not even sticking up for me a little. I hate that he's going to the dance with Clare. I really, really hate Clare. Looking at him, his longish, streaky hair somehow managing to shine without sun, his legs looking newly hairy, I think I still love him. Yep, I do. Is he really approaching me?

He's got his baseball hat on sideways. His friends drop their skateboards to the ground, nod goodbyes, and fluidly glide ahead of him. As they pass me I hear a faint "Whad' up" come from Jake, one of the beautiful skater boys James hangs out with. I nod, but he's already slid by.

James is now in front of me. Oh god, I can't even look him in the eye. My humiliation is like a breathing animal standing between us. I can almost see it. I know he feels its presence too. I concentrate on a spot just above and to the left of his right shoulder.

"Oh, hey, James." My voice quavers. This is awful.

"Mattie, hey. What're you doing out here alone at night? I mean, not that it's *that* late . . ."

"*You* guys are out here, and we're the same age." I must turn this so-called conversation back to him. And I think I sound just the right amount of casual-not-nervous-quick-thinking.

James drops his skateboard and puts one unlaced shoe on it. He rolls it back and forth, back and forth, arms folded across his chest.

"Yeah, true."

We stand there, no one saying anything. He keeps sliding his board back and forth, as though waiting for me to speak. I am pretty much concentrating on just remaining alive at this point. My mouth and brain no longer recall the skill of speech.

James shrugs and expertly flips the board up by stomping on the back of it. He nimbly catches it, vertically from the top, and balances it on the toe of his shoe. He looks out across the bay, squinting at a huge tanker. He swings his head between that and a distant barge that seems to be lingering near Treasure Island. I watch him watching them. I am looking indirectly, trying to make my eyes slide slowly so it doesn't look like I'm staring.

"Okay, well." He looks back to me. I perk an eyebrow. (I have perfected the one-eyebrow-raised ability in the mirror. It conveys, I hope, "Yes, do go on . . .")

It must have worked. He coughs, starts talking again without looking at me. "My great aunt just died and my parents are meeting with some dude about her funeral. They're at his house, which I guess is the funeral home too." James turns and points to the arc of houses that peel off the bay into strips of small streets. "It's creepy to have a funeral home be where you sleep and stuff." He yawns, and glances briefly at me before resuming his squinting at the barge. "They, I mean my parents, can see this trail from the guy's living room, so they said I could ride the loop once and then come back."

James is totally talking to me. I mean he's telling me about his personal life. This is unbelievable. Do I dare believe he doesn't really think I am a total idiot?

I nod and say, too excitedly, "Wow . . . you know my friend Ariel?" I pause, wondering if he knows who she is.

"Oh yeah, I know who she is." He coughs a little, blushes. I realize Ariel's probably known to every boy in junior high because of her impressively large chest, not to mention the hydrant-red hair that announces her wherever she goes. Maybe the spell will make that better too. She wants to meet boys, but not because she's a 32D.

"Well anyway, this is so weird, I mean because of your aunt," (good god, I am babbling). "See, Ariel has a neighbor who just died this week too."

James nods. A huge fat lady with the tiniest dog I have ever seen walks by us slowly. The dog shakes and boings like a hyper chicken. Its legs are no bigger around than one of my fingers and it's dressed in a red and beige plaid sweater with a silver buckle. The massive woman eyeballs James's skateboard and gives us both a look of disgust.

James smiles at her fakely and says, "Cute hamster you got there!"

The woman rolls her eyes at him and continues on, dragging the silly animal behind her. It looks back at us and quivers, as though it knows we have made fun of it.

"That was funny!" I smile and actually manage to make eye contact. "I always think of something like that to say but either not in time, or I just don't have the nerve to actually say what I think of." It's official, I am the babble queen.

James shrugs, resumes with the back-and-forth-skateboard-under-the-shoe motion. Must be a nervous habit or something. More silence. I need to say something, keep him talking.

"I never knew anyone that died, so this is weird. I mean, of course I didn't know your aunt, and I didn't really know know Mrs. Rosencrantz . . ."

James head snaps up, his skateboard is stilled under the hard thud of his shoe. "What did you say?"

Oh god, my mouth has diarrhea. I am making no sense. "Doesn't matter, really. Just, I meant I never have really gone *through death* . . ."

"No, about Mrs. Rosencrantz."

"Mrs. Rosencrantz?"

"That *is* what you said!"

I am confused. "Uh, yeah, she's Ariel's neighbor. She's the old lady who died. . . ."

"And SHE is my great aunt."

I am stunned. I stare at him, and realize my mouth is probably hanging slack and stupid. It's all hard to put together for a second.

"Mrs. Rosencrantz!" He says it impatiently, as though helping a small, dumb child grasp something basic.

"Wow, this is the hugest coincidence." I shake my head and give James what I hope is a look of intrigue and connection.

"So you knew her, huh?"

"Yes! Well, not really, I mean, just sort of. She always used to . . . talk to us, and to Ariel and her family, all the time. She was very friendly. She was nice." None of us ever had one "nice" thing to say about Mrs. Rosencrantz, but I can't say that to James. I mean, this is his relative.

"She was strange, and we didn't see her that much." He shrugs, reseats his hat on his head.

"Oh."

"Weird that you knew her. And Ariel too. Huh." He stares at the barge again, which is moving out, curving right toward open ocean. "Well I better go. See ya around."

"Oh, yeah, okay, bye James. Thanks for stopping to talk." I can't believe I just said that. As though I am so lucky that he did (even though I am) . . . it sounds so desperate.

"Whatever." He shrugs, drops his skateboard to the ground. "You going to go the funeral? Maybe with Ariel?"

"Umm, well, I don't know . . . ," but James hasn't waited for my answer. He gives me a wrist flip that I will optimistically call a wave and he's off. I watch as he expertly avoids a Skater before disappearing around the long curve in the trail.

I feel deflated, off balance, unreal. I don't know if I can do the ritual anymore. The angry bravery that was my fuel is gone. I suddenly think of kidnappers. I think of falling into the dirty, cold water of the bay and drowning, no one around to hear me calling out. I think of the trinkets, sealed in muck all these months, corroding, rotting, becoming fragments. I should leave them be.

I should go home. I need to go be safe. I need to think. About James. About Mrs. Rosencrantz, about my mother, and about my friends. Surely James was put in my path tonight to stop me from undoing the ritual. Maybe I've been deceiving myself, maybe tonight ISN'T the night. I am sooo confused, but happy, and exhausted.

I cross the trail and walk the ten steps it takes to reach the damp sand. Seagulls, even at night, circle and cry hopefully above me. Everyone feeds them old bread here on this stretch of beach. I want to shout at them that I have nothing. I don't even have a clue, let alone a moldy hot dog bun. The lights of San Francisco are beautiful. I turn my back on the million lights and start toward home.

Mom Is Coming Home

I wake up. Immediately I feel a vague, unformed worry collect in my temples. I can't put reason to it. It takes me a full minute to shake off the mucky numbness of a deep sleep and remember . . . fighting with Ariel and Nicki, Mom being gone, James. Spells and never-done rituals, dying babies and dead old ladies. All of it. I wish I had slept longer.

I lie in my bed for a full hour. I replay yesterday. I have had whole years of life pass and less has happened within some of them than all that happened in yesterday's single-day span. I try and sort out little bits—like planning what to say to Ariel, or how to talk to Mom when she comes home, but I can't focus on any one piece of my life. It all tumbles together and into one big, massive problem. My life.

I hear a cupboard slam from the kitchen. Aunt

Winda. I can't stand just lying here and torturing myself with all this thought, so I decide to get up. I swing my legs out of bed. My right foot crunches down on something squeaky and slick. A small clamshell container left from last night. I grab it up in disgust and smash it between my palms. Teriyaki sauce drips out. I mash the brown dots of syrupy stuff into the carpet with my toe. I stash the ruined container on my shelf behind a particularly large pig figurine. I guess my pigs are good for something once in awhile.

In the kitchen Aunt Winda is making muffins. Again. I realize suddenly it is the only food I have ever seen her make. She looks sad and tired.

"Hey, Auntie." I cross the kitchen and flop down in a chair. "Care if I have coffee?"

She waves a limp hand toward the machine. "Yeah, go ahead, knock yourself out."

I don't need to be asked twice, and I grab a mug and pour. I love the smell, the taste, and the not unpleasing effects of liquid caffeine.

"We're going to get your mom this morning. If you want to shower or anything first . . ."

"Did you talk to her already this morning?"

"Yeah. She said everything was fine. This was a huge thing for her, not coming home last night. You can imagine she's anxious to get back home . . ."

"We'll leave in an hour." Aunt Winda peers into the oven at the muffins.

"Do I need to go with you?"

Aunt Winda looks startled. "I guess not, Miss M. But don't you want to? Your mom, I think, expects you to."

"I 'expected' her to be home yesterday too. Not that it really mattered, but you know what I mean. Anyway, I was going to go over to Ariel's."

"Again?"

Oops. I forgot I was supposedly over there last night already.

I sip at my coffee, look at her in a "you can never possibly understand what I go through" sort of way. I don't know why, but I always go into the bratty kid routine around my aunt. I'm usually not so smart mouthed. But I really do want to go over to Ariel's, and I think she'll agree because of (or maybe despite?) my whining.

Aunt Winda rubs her thumb up and down the silver zipper of her green hooded jacket, staring at me. I can tell she's not sure how to handle this.

"Look, Mom just wants to come straight home, right? It's not like we're going to do anything except just sit in the car. I'll be here when you get back and talk to her then . . ." Aunt Winda is staring at me as I speak, her mouth in a tight line. It makes little, frowny parentheses at the corners.

She sighs, runs her fingers through her hair. Nods, finally. "Okay, Miss M, okay." I win.

She turns away and again checks the muffins. They're done and she grabs the pan with a pig pot holder. I got it when I was nine, along with a matching apron. That was in the days before Dad left, when he used to ask me to help him in the kitchen. The pig pattern, once bright primary colors, is faded and stained with years of kitchen grease. It looks like the pigs, holding rolling pins and leaning over steaming pies, are behind some sort of blurry glass. They look worn down. Not unlike Aunt Winda looks this morning. Not unlike I feel these days.

I blow Aunt Winda a kiss when she leaves and head to my room. I am going to go over to Ariel's without calling. I need to tell her about all that happened last night. I hope she's not still mad or sulking about our disagreement. Maybe Nicki can come over too.

Betrayal

Ariel's not there. Her brother answers the door. He's eating an apple and doesn't bother to finish chewing as he tells me she was going for a walk with some guy. I pretend to be unsurprised. I am actually shocked. Ariel, *with a guy?* I try to get more information out of her brother, but he knows nothing more and watching him talk around all that chewed-up apple is disgusting.

I don't want to go back home and just sit there. Mom won't be home for at least an hour. I decide to walk the trail for awhile. I want to revisit the spot where James and I talked.

Sunny Saturdays along the main island's trail are bustling and cheerful. There are always lots of people walking, riding, sitting in the sand, feeding the birds. I want to be around that right now.

There are some kids clumped together on the sand, laughing. I crane my head to see what's so funny.

There, mashed into a little mound of sand, is a seagull couple. They're doing it. I mean, having sex. The female struggles against him, but he holds her hard with his beak clamped into her neck feathers. I am horrified and fascinated. I feel a rush of blood to my face. I am also really embarrassed, but I watch anyway.

One boy, he looks about ten, says, "They are screwing," and throws a stick at them. It makes me mad, the mean-spirited stick throwing, but I am relieved to see the male seagull release the poor bird beneath him. She scuttles away quickly, crying and cawing the whole time, as if lecturing the other bird for his rude behavior. The dumb boy throws another stick at the male, who quickly darts out of its way and flies off.

The kids drift apart, breaking into pairs and ambling along the water's edge. I look up the curving trail and see a familiar spot of color. Spiky red hair. Ariel! I hadn't seen her before because of the densely packed kids watching the seagulls. She's sitting with someone on one of the benches but I am too far away to see their faces clearly.

I start toward her and soon I am close enough for their features to become distinct. I stop walking suddenly, right in the middle of the trail. An angry bicyclist yells at me to move to the side. I can't move though. I really can't.

It's James. She's sitting with James. He has one hand on the skateboard propped beside him, and the other is draped over the back of the bench. Over Ariel's shoulders in fact. He basically has his arm around her. I stare. They are talking so intently, looking at each other so closely, they don't see me.

I feel like something is sitting on my chest. It won't allow air to enter my lungs. A high-pitched ringing blossoms in my ears. I feel a soup of body chemicals surge into my system. I guess this is the "fight-or-flight" reaction we studied in biology. It works, saves me, and my chest expands with air. I am supercharged with physical energy. My legs begin an instant sprint. It's flight all right, fueled by the raw shock. I run fast, faster than I ever have, away from them.

Bay of Pigs

I am breathing so hard I sound like I have asthma.
It takes me three tries to get my key in the lock. I go
straight to my room. The house is empty and quiet. I
throw myself on my floor, face down. Strangely, I am
not crying. My eyes feel hot, but they are dry. It hits
me: I am not devastated, I am *pissed*. I mean, *how
could she?*

I lay like that for awhile, mashing my nose and forehead into the carpet and letting the anger form a nice
protective shell around the bleeding part inside me.
For some reason I keep flashing back to the seagulls,
the way the female's eyes rolled back as the male bit
into her neck.

I become aware of the intermittent beep of the
answering machine. It means there's a message. I get
up to play it. Also, I am incredibly thirsty.

I grab a water bottle from the fridge and chug it fast. I get brain freeze for a second. I toss the bottle into the recycling and grab another before heading into the living room. I push the blinking message light. The phone's lady-zombie voice tells me I have one new message.

"Hey M, it's Mom. Just wanted you to know that we won't be home until later today. I'm . . ."—here she stutters, becomes quieter—"I'm . . . not ready to come home right this second. I mean I'm not quite up to the trip out . . . to the *getting* back. But later today, okay? I want to be home, see *you*. Anyway, you're at Ariel's now I guess, so if you get this and want to go back to her house, leave a note. We'll call you there. I mean later today, when we're back." She sighs, pauses. I hear Aunt Winda saying something in the background. "Sorry honey, I love you and we'll talk tonight, okay?" It sounds as if she is going to say something more. I hear that little intake of air sound that she makes before speaking, but the machine beeps, cuts her off, and there are no more words.

I finish the second bottle of water and throw it on the floor. I kick it and watch it skitter across the floor and hit the wall. I don't know what to do with myself. I try to call Nicki, but her phone goes to voicemail and I hang up.

Back in my room, I sit on my bed. I have mounds of homework to do. For the first time ever I am not doing great in school, and also for the first time I don't really care. I can't concentrate on homework. I stare at the pigs. They stare back.

I pick up the pig music box my dad gave me last year. It plays *Farmer in the Dell* when you wind the little curly tail sticking out of the side. It is so dumb. I hold it above my wooden table and I drop it. It smashes spectacularly. The little piano thing that makes the music plays a few broken notes.

Next I snatch up a snow globe my mom gave me when I was really little. Back when I liked pigs. Inside there is a tiny, little table set with white plates and lots of little pigs sitting on benches around it. They have red and white checkered napkins tied around their necks and they hold crude-looking wooden spoons in their hooves. A mother pig in an apron holds a little wooden bowl and the father pig smokes a pipe at the other end of the table. I used to love looking at this little scene, imagining all the work someone put into carving the teeny, little things inside the globe. I even named the pig children, and as I stare into their miniature world I still remember each name. Beth is the oldest pig child. She looks thoughtfully across the table at Larry and Stuart, who are clearly toddler-aged twin pigs. To Beth's left is Ben, a teenage pig who wears a serious expression. Lastly, there's Alice May, the baby of the family, sitting on a tiny, carved booster seat and beaming her piglet smile at her mother.

When it hits the table it only cracks. Water leaks out and drips off the table. The second time it breaks into three large pieces. The pig family, apparently all attached permanently to each other, lands upright and continues to wait calmly for dinner.

I work my way through everything that can be broken. Glass, plastic, thin wood, stained glass, ceramic. Several pigs are surprisingly stubborn about their destruction and repeated falls from high up are required. The fragile pigs fare the worst. The tough ones—the heavy carvings of metal or thick wood—I just throw on the floor. At last my shelves are empty. I remember the picture Dad gave me recently and scrape it out from under my bed. The glass shatters easily, and the frame breaks into four even pieces.

I stare in wonder at what I've done. There are pieces of pig everywhere. Glass and shards of ceramic litter my table and floor. There are wet patches from the snow globe. Straw stuffing from one pig popped out when I ripped his tail off and it sticks to the damp table. My carpet sparkles like a land of strange crystals.

I am glad I didn't take my shoes off when I got home. I carefully walk across the ruin and into the hallway. I sit with my back against the wall, gazing into my room. As I stare at what I've done, something from the spell book pops into my mind. It said the most powerful rituals require great sacrifice. We thought when we buried our objects and recited the poem of change that *those* things were a sacrifice. But they weren't. Not really. Our sacrifices weren't real enough and now we are being punished. They didn't mean enough to us and we wouldn't truly miss them. Our sacrifices weren't real enough and now we are being punished. It seems so clear to me.

But these pigs meant a lot, though a lot of it is bad. They have been with me all my life. I remember who gave me each object, how old I was. They have watched me sleep and seen me grow. I have sacrificed all of them now. I need to make it count for something. I have an unshakeable feeling that I can set everything right, that this is my moment.

I go into the kitchen to get a broom and dustpan. I grab my mom's yellow dish gloves from under the sink. Carefully, I collect all the bits and pieces of pig in a canvas bag. I end up needing two bags to hold everything. I'll have to vacuum and dust well to get it really clean, but I don't have time right now.

I am excited to haul them out to the bay. I anticipate a cleansed, hopeful feeling when I watch the bags sink into the mucky water. I never stopped believing in the magic of rituals and spells, even if my friends did. This sacrifice will set things right. It's got to. I can't tolerate the thought that it won't.

I Have the Fake Flu
and Mom Is on Drugs

I try to look ill by patting my water-dampened hands all over my face and rubbing my eyes hard to make them look red. Mom is still in bed when I shuffle into her room. She turns over groggily.

"Morning, honey. I'm getting up in a second." She stretches and sighs.

"I feel rotten, Mom. I'm staying home." Normally I would ask to stay home and proceed to list my symptoms, each of which Mom would try to verify by looking in my throat, feeling my forehead, etc., and then she would pronounce my fate about going to school. Now I am *telling* her.

She notices and sits up. She squints at me. "You're sick?"

"Uh-huh. Feel lousy. I think I have the flu."

She nods her head slowly, still staring at me. "All right M, but no TV, and no computer either. I have two complicated claims that need to be processed so I'll need the computer all day."

"Fine, I'll just sleep. Maybe read." I try to sound frail, though the act is not necessary since obviously she's letting me stay home.

She flops back down. Her hair falls limply on her pillow and it looks greasy. Apparently she didn't wash it when she was at Winda's, and I know she didn't shower when she finally got home last night. "I'm going to lie here another few minutes." She turns on her side and curls into herself, hugging her pillow. "Let me know if you need anything."

"Sure, Mom." I turn away, leaving her in the musty-smelling nest of messy blankets and worn throw pillows.

I am not sick at all, of course. In fact, I feel so full of energy I'll probably have to do sit-ups and jumping jacks in my room to burn off some of it. I can't face Ariel, that's why I am staying home. Or James.

James.

I wonder if she would tell me about James if I talked to her (which I will not), or if eventually I'll have to see them, maybe holding hands or something, in the halls at school. Anyway, I just can't face it yet. Besides, all the broken pigs, now sunk in the bay, need time to create some magic. Every time I notice my empty shelves I feel a stab of panic, but also a surge of hope.

Back in my room I spend the morning looking at my stack of old *Teen* magazines. I try a bunch of hairstyles I see on the models and experiment with makeup, though I don't really wear makeup so much yet. When I do go back to school I want to look cool, collected, and pretty. Maybe older. Definitely different.

I picture the new me with streaked hair and wearing mascara every day. Some girls in my grade do. Clare does. Then again, Clare's already got a body like a Victoria's Secret model. Seventh grade is one of those times you really notice the truth in the "we all develop and grow uniquely" line adults are always chanting. I finally give up, wash my face and throw my hair into a ponytail.

I am bored. I wander into the kitchen for something to eat, and I see Mom quickly switch her screen from RollerCoaster Tycoon to her work stuff. She swivels toward me.

"How're you feeling?"

"Better I guess. I'm hungry."

"That's good. I did an online order today from Safeway. They're delivering tomorrow. Until then, there isn't much to eat." Her brow furrows in worry.

"I'll eat peanut butter, Mom, it's fine."

She nods. "I know I should just go grocery shopping, M. I know. Give me time."

I shrug, say nothing. She turns back to her "work" and I start rummaging for food.

Mom and Aunt Winda finally got home about seven last night. She looked exhausted and old as we sat together on the couch and she gave me a speech that had obviously been planned and rehearsed. It was very Dr. Phil. Basically she told me she was depressed and anxious (duh) and that this depression-slash-anxiety was "manifesting" as introversion. She asked me if I knew what "manifest" and "introversion" meant. I just rolled my eyes and told her, "Yeah, and I even have a handle on 'agoraphobia.'" Neither my attitude nor my use of the word seemed to surprise her.

The middle part of her speech involved telling me it wasn't my fault, or my dad's fault, and that I shouldn't blame anyone. Yadda yadda. Her conclusion focused on how she would get better. She planned to see the therapist once a week, which would force her out of the house and on a long trip (I deserve credit for not pointing out that going to San Francisco is not exactly a long trip—I could practically swim there if the water wasn't freezing). And she's started taking some medication called Klonopin. She talked about anxiety disorders and panic attacks and shame. I listened and heard nothing surprising.

Like any good presentation, after it was given she opened up the floor for questions. I didn't have any. I told her I was glad that she would figure out how to go shopping again and I went to my room. I felt mean. She didn't follow me. I heard her murmuring with Aunt

Winda. I washed my face and brushed my teeth and went to bed early.

Amazingly, she doesn't know my pigs are gone. She hasn't come in my room since she got home. I don't know what I'll say when she finds out. I certainly can't tell her I broke them all and threw them in the bay in an effort to change my life. It sounds crazy, even to me, when it's said like that. But it isn't crazy.

I take a sandwich and a glass of water back to my room. I really wanted milk, but there isn't any. The phone rings twice, and Mom answers it. I hear her coming down the hall. Quickly I scoot into the hall-way, closing my door behind me, as if I'm going to the bathroom.

"Phone, M. It's Nicki. She's calling from the hospital ..."

Her brother's surgery! With everything that's been going on, I totally forgot it was today. I grab the phone, ignoring my mother's look of question, and go back in my room.

"Nicki?"

We All Meet at Nicki's House

Her brother couldn't be fixed. That's exactly what
the doctors had said. Like he was an old lawn mower
or something. He's not going to die immediately or
anything, but it's not good. Nicki, in her gentle way,
is mourning already. Everything about her seems sad.
Her hair is droopy and her normally glowing skin is
yellowish and raw around her mouth.

We are sitting in Nicki's room. The three of us
have gathered here for the first time ever. I had to
make a somewhat miraculous recovery from my fake
flu to convince my mom to let me come. Nicki said
she needed company, and we would finally see her
house, so there was no way I would miss the chance.
I told her about Nicki's brother and that sad bit of
information was enough for her to let me go without
further whining.

Nicki called Ariel too. Ariel came straight from school and got here at the same time I did. We have not spoken directly to each other yet. We're carefully keeping Nicki between us. Physically and in the other ways.

I am sitting in a rocking chair with a suede, butt-shaped seat that is incredibly comfortable. Nicki's room is big and kind of, well, not girl's-room-like. It's more like a living room or something. Besides the chair I am sitting in, there's a little love seat thing with an ottoman. They're covered in coarse material with big flowers in browns and watery oranges. On her floor she has one of those braided circle rugs. There are three framed photographs of trees and a lake hung in a grouping on her main wall.

There are no posters or calendars, no piles of rejected clothes in a heap on the floor. No used cups or glasses. Her small desk shines with wax. There are no messy papers and books jumbled together, only a neat, little desk organizer holding sharpened pencils, a stapler, and some colored paper clips. It makes me feel off center and confused somehow . . . all this neatness and order. Her bed is even made.

"Miss M! Are you even listening?" Ariel's angry voice interrupts my thoughts. I guess I had been studying Nicki's room so intently, rocking back and forth in the comfy chair, that I had spaced out. Plus, Ariel hadn't talked to me yet (and I certainly hadn't talked to her either), so I hadn't tuned in to her voice. Why would I?

This whole thing between us is just gaining momentum. I guess anger can do that, just grow and expand on its own. Mine has. Hers has too apparently, which is ridiculous. I mean, I am the injured party here, but however things have developed and shifted in Ariel's head, she is acting mad at me. She's been stewing about the sleepover night when we argued, but that's nothing compared to my issue with her. I haven't told her about seeing her with James yet.

I can't wait to spring it on her, see her shock, and watch her squirm around making excuses. I am waiting now like a predator, ready to pounce. I can already picture Nicki's horror and disgust when she hears what a traitor Ariel is.

I slowly turn my head toward her and give her a blank look. She stares back.

"Look, M, let's just stop this, okay?" She's looking down now. She's sitting on the ottoman cross-legged. She looks like a little girl, sitting drooped over like that. Except for the chest of course. That shelf of flesh James's hand, my James's hand was inches from on that bench.

"Stop what?" I say in my most sarcastic voice. I hear Nicki expel a sigh of worry.

Ariel looks up at me and I see her eyes are shiny with the threat of tears. "M, just, come on. I'm sorry about the other night. I think we both acted kind of wrong. You just made me so mad, pushing us to do that ritual. I mean, we have to face it, that our lives can't be fixed by sneaking around at night digging holes by the bay!"

I shrug, act indifferent. I turn back to Nicki. "Nicki, we're here for you right now, to talk about your brother. Ariel and I don't need to do this, now . . ." I am so righteous. The I-will-pounce-soon feeling is becoming stronger.

Nicki stands up and walks over to her bed. She straightens the already perfectly straight duvet, smoothing the thin white material with her long brown fingers. She sits carefully on the edge. "No, I want you guys to talk now. Be done with this silly fighting. I told you everything about my brother, there's nothing more to say. He'll come home sometime next week. Truthfully, I knew you guys would come if I called. And I thought it would force you together. To sort this out."

I can't believe Nicki has manipulated us like this! I didn't know she had it in her. I am annoyed but also strangely pleased that my quiet friend is so secretly crafty.

"Well, I am *trying* to talk to her . . . ," Ariel tells Nicki.

"I miss you two . . . us three. Come on, Mattie, don't be stubborn! You and Ariel *together* keep me going. I need you to make up!" Nicki sounds desperate now.

I look around her room, think about how much more there is learn about her, what a short period of time it has been since she became our third best friend. I really care about Nicki by now, and obviously Ariel and I are important to her too. The fact of our friendship strikes me, and I feel just a tiny bit less like murdering Ariel. But only a tiny bit.

I start rocking again slowly. I let my head fall back against the wood of the chair so I am looking up at the ceiling. I say it slowly, keeping my voice low and flat. I speak with a heavy pause between every word. I will admit to building the drama on purpose. But it's dramatic news. I rock back and forth to the exact beat of my words.

"I'm sorry, Nicki, but I can't really forgive Ariel. And it's not about the ritual or the sleepover. It's about James. Ariel, I saw you with him. I *saw* you." I continue to rock, but now I am staring hard at Ariel.

Ariel bursts into tears.

Reunited

As I hear Ariel out, I am forced to admit that I was totally wrong. Now I feel like such a fool. I mean, I should have known that Ariel, my best, loyal friend since we were tiny, would never go after a guy I liked. And she didn't.

See, it happened like this: James called her and asked if she would go for a walk with him to talk about me. He said he felt really bad about me thinking he was asking me to the dance. He said Clare was kinda mean, and he wanted to make it all right. He thought Ariel could talk to me for him (and right then I remembered that he had asked all about *Ariel* when I had seen him that evening by the bay). In hindsight, maybe I did smell a rat, or a fish, or whatever, right then. I mean, hello, can you say set-up?

He also told Ariel he heard she was Mrs. Rosencrantz's neighbor and said that she was his aunt. He said he'd love to hear some stories about being her neighbor. He acted crushed, Ariel said, by Mrs. Rosencrantz's death. I couldn't believe it. He'd told me the night before that he barely knew his aunt and thought she was strange.

Anyway, Ariel had walked out to the path to meet him. He had asked her all about Mrs. Rosencrantz, but (and here Ariel gave me a little worried frown of sympathy) every time Ariel brought me up he changed the subject. He said he had a leg cramp and luckily there was a bench to sit on. The bench I saw them on. He sat too close, Ariel said, and it had made her uncomfortable. She scooched to the edge (and I do remember, now, she was sitting all the way to one side of the bench).

She said it all felt weird and wrong at that point. He didn't talk about me, and he was acting odd. She decided to go home. She said, just as she told him she needed to get going, she felt his hand brush the top of her boob. It startled her—she hadn't noticed that his arm had crept behind and over her—and she had jumped up. I must have seen them and run off just before this happened. If only I'd stayed a little longer and not assumed the worst!

She said she was about to just go, get away, when she spotted two of James's skateboarding friends across the path peeking over a sand dune. They were rubbing their chests in circles and high-fiving. They stopped immediately when Ariel spotted them, but it was enough. She had been set up, made a fool of, again, because of her chest. She hadn't said anything, just walked away.

Ariel is crying by the end of the story. Nicki hugs her and makes little shushing noises. I rock and weep too. I feel all these separate bubbles of emotion welling inside me. Anger at myself for assuming Ariel and James had a thing, and at James for being such a jerk. Disappointment, because I *liked* James, and seeing him for what he really is—a boob-grabbing jerk—means I can't anymore. Pain, for Ariel, who was used like that. Relief, because I have Ariel back, and she never left me after all. All these bubbles fill me so full I can hardly breathe.

All three of us come together, in the middle of Nicki's room. We hug and cry. We tumble over each other talking, apologizing, making little jokes. We are back together, we three, and I am thankful.

At last we settle down. Ariel starts talking about her letter to Rachael Ray, and suddenly it hits me . . . I burst into fresh tears. Who knew a body could produce endless tears? Apparently the body of a thirteen-year-old girl can.

Ariel stops in the middle of a sentence, not understanding my seemingly unrelated burst of crying. "M? You're so *upset . . .*"

I hiccup a little and draw a shaky breath. "I forgot

for awhile, or maybe I just ignored the truth. But, well, it just hit me when you started talking about the letter. See, I did something awful. I was so mad. I was just thinking about James, and Mom, and not being able to talk to you guys. What I've done, it can't be fixed."

Nicki comes over to me, pats my back. "Mattie, maybe it can be . . ."

"No! It can't! I destroyed all my pigs. Every one of them. I threw the pieces in the bay."

"What?" Ariel sounds confused, and Nicki's expression mimes Ariel's tone.

"I broke them all. Into pieces. I hold my hands up, cupping an imaginary pig, and whoosh my hands down. They both watch the imaginary pig fall and shatter. They get it.

"Oh, Miss M." Ariel sounds like she's in church, her voice is so quiet.

I think of all those jagged pieces of pig, how they looked scattered across my floor. For the first time, it hits me how permanent it is.

But my friends are here, back with me now, and that is something. A big something. Now what will I do?

Three Girls, One New Attitude

A few weeks have passed since we all made up. We have been inseparable at school, and we have a new attitude. We don't avoid Clare's pack or James anymore. We walk by, heads up, even smiling at them. We had planned how we would act, how we would show James he meant nothing. We decided the best revenge would be to act totally untouched by all of it. And we are enjoying it, even though it feels like playacting sometimes, this outgoing attitude we pretend to have. Actually, it is feeling more real all the time. It's a funny thing . . . I didn't realize how hard we worked to be invisible until we stopped doing it.

We went to Mrs. Rosencrantz's funeral last Tuesday. Ariel's mom was going to go, then Ariel decided to go with her, but she didn't want to go without us. It was my first funeral. I didn't have the courage to look into the open casket. I will admit it was very creepy. I could see the tip of Mrs. Rosencrantz's nose and the plastic frames of her glasses from my seat, and that was enough.

The whole thing was like a play to me. Death is a little unreal. Honestly, I don't really get death. I don't accept it. James sat in the front pew with the other relatives. He caught sight of us for a second, when we first came in, but acted like he didn't see us. Fine.

Actually, as wrong as this probably is given we were at his aunt's funeral, it felt good to know we were making *him* uncomfortable. Since the funeral, it has been easy for us to act so . . . so . . . untouched. It's like pretending to be so tough is making us that way for real. At least a little.

We are eating lunch at a table in the middle of the quad today. No one is sitting at "our" rinky table by the temporary building, but in keeping with our new out-thereness, we decided to grab more central real estate. The murmur of other huddles of kids, talking and eating, is pleasant. It is new, this feeling we have of being in the middle of things, not off to the side.

Clare and the beautiful ones are two tables to our left. They are a tangle of tanned legs, sparkling earrings, and loud chatter. You can tell all the boys register the table—they all sort of lean toward it, with eyes or gestures. I know we'll never really be like them, or friends with them. It's okay though.

Lunch is going to be a big deal today, at least for Ariel. She hands us each a stuffed tomato. Each of the vegetables (or are they fruits?) is packed in its own round, plastic container, the kind with the built-in ice thing you freeze beforehand. She gives us each a small paper plate, a pack of plastic silverware, and a paper napkin along with the container.

She made the tomatoes last night, one for each of us. They are an impossible red (hothouse grown, she told us), and stuffed with fresh flaked tuna, capers, fresh tarragon, and a dab of homemade mayonnaise. The recipe is something she created and plans to enter in a contest. She called me and Nicki last night, saying she thought she'd perfected the recipe and wanted us to try it. So now we are.

I slice a wedge of tomato with my plastic knife, mashing the flakes of tuna into the flesh before putting the bite in my mouth. Capers look like mouse poop, but I wisely say nothing about this observation. I chew thoughtfully. We promised to be brutally honest about the taste. Ariel watches me anxiously. As always, Nicki is waiting to try hers until she knows I haven't gagged or keeled over.

I swallow and make an exaggerated throat-clearing noise before speaking. Then I use my most snobby voice: "The tuna is like butter; light and soft against my tongue. The zap of salt from the capers is a pleasant and refreshing contrast. The savory herb blend brings out the natural tanginess of the tomato." I gaze upward and squint at the sky in exaggerated contemplation. Then I level my gaze at Ariel and say, "It's simply mah-ve-lus!"

Nicki bursts out laughing and Ariel giggles. "Okay, M, very funny. Obviously I've exposed you to too many cooking shows. You've certainly got the lingo down! But seriously, do you like it?"

"Ariel, my little mermaid, it is really good. Seriously." And I mean it.

She smiles and takes a breath of relief.

Nicki is trying hers now too. She gives Ariel a thumbs-up and stuffs another huge wedge in her mouth.

"Are you going to send it to Rachael?" I ask Ariel between bites.

"Yeah, I think so. She said to take my time, but I think the recipe's ready. Besides, I just want a clean slate. I want this whole thing to be behind me."

Rachael Ray actually wrote back to Ariel. She was really cool about it, but she did say what Ariel did was wrong, of course. She told Ariel to write to Pillsbury and withdraw the recipe immediately. Rachael also said a good chef relies on creativity and originality, and she challenged Ariel to come up with her own original recipe. She said she'd cook it herself and review it, and if it was *excellent,* all would be forgiven.

Ariel wrote Pillsbury the letter saying it had come to her attention that the scone recipe wasn't exactly original. She didn't say it was a Rachael Ray recipe, just that it wasn't hers. She sent the check back with VOID written in black Sharpie across it, just as Rachael had told her to do.

She hasn't heard back yet, and is still nervous about what might happen, but she feels way better now. Ariel's parents still don't know about any of it. She doesn't plan to ever tell them either, and hopefully she will never have to.

All in all, the day goes by pleasantly after lunch. As I walk home, my thoughts drift from Ariel to something a bit more interesting at the moment. I am thinking about this guy, Brad, who is in my history class. I don't know why I never noticed him before. He's quiet, but very cute if you stop and really look. He has that kind of hair that sticks up in little spikes above his forehead. He wears a necklace with a real shark's tooth on a leather cord.

He moved to Alameda this year, but I don't know where from. I need a new crush. I do believe we have a candidate in Brad. I am trying to remember his last name (Garvey? Garson? Something with a G . . .) as I walk into my house. I am so in my own head I don't notice for a few seconds that my mom is sitting on the floor in the middle of the living room. Tears run down her face. Her legs stick out awkwardly and she has her hands fisted together between them.

"Oh, Matilda, what have you done?"

The Pig Massacre Is Discovered by Mom

I drop my backpack. Stare at her. Her dull hair and gray, frayed T-shirt disgust me. I do one of those head-pulled-back, nose-wrinkle looks designed to make a person feel like they are being incomprehensible.

"Oh, Miss M. What happened to all your pigs?"

So that's it. After weeks, weeks, she has finally gone in my room and actually noticed the bare shelves. I shrug my shoulders.

"Please tell me you packed them up, that they're . . . somewhere . . ." She makes circles with her wrists indicating our house.

"Okay, Mom, I'll tell you. I *did* pack them up. But they happened to all be in broken pieces when I did. And they are somewhere . . . the bottom of the bay." I feel so quick witted and mean. My sarcasm is impeccable.

Mom shakes her head back and forth slowly. "Oh, honey, no," she seems to be talking to herself, "your pigs. All those memories, those trips and birthdays . . ."

"They were fake *pigs* mom. NOT memories and trips. I stopped liking them years ago. Did you know that?"

She's shaking her head back and forth, staring at me, searching my eyes. I don't like it; I feel so mad that she can look *into* me like that.

"Miss M . . . Matilda . . . honey, why?"

"Why not, Mom? I was sick of them, okay?" I grab my backpack and head to my room, purposely ignoring her begging me to stay and talk about it.

I flop on my bed. The truth is that I have regretted destroying all the pigs for awhile now. I even started a journal about them. On each page I sketch one pig from the collection and write about when and how I got it. I have remembered stuff I forgot. Like the trip when my dad took us to Death Valley (plastic molded pig holding a sign that said "Death Valley or Bust"), the birthday I had on Angel Island in third grade (ceramic pig with wire halo and wings from Ariel), and the time Aunt Winda took me to the HoneyBaked Ham store (cardboard pig with word bubble: "now with maple glaze"), where we stood in line for an hour. She had amused me by making finger animals and doing little plays.

The truth is, my mom is right. The pigs *are* memories: trips, holidays, parties, sicknesses, surprises, and all that. They are, or were, each a chapter in my life, a way to look back and see all the different me's I have been. I've destroyed them, and I realize I've taken something vast and unnameable away from myself.

I have decided not to dwell though, so I call Ariel. She's bored. I tell her about Brad. She remembers his last name is Griswold. We three-way call Nicki, and she's bored too. We decide to meet at Nicki's and do something together.

I leave quickly, telling Mom I am going to Nicki's. She doesn't look up from her Tycooning and try to stop me. I let the door bang extra hard, hoping she'll at least reprimand me like always, but all I hear is the click of the keyboard.

Noah's Cute, Mom's Insane

Nicki seems to want us to come to her house all the time now, as though making up for all those months we didn't. Ariel and I are fine with it too. Nicki's dad likes cooking and they have a really cool kitchen. Ariel about passed out on the floor when she saw the convection oven, six-burner gas stove, and all the doodads perched on roll-out shelves beneath the granite counter. It is so obvious she would kill to cook in that kitchen, but she is waiting for Nicki to ask her to. She has been dropping hints, but so far Nicki hasn't invited her to cook anything.

Ariel's already in Nicki's room when I get there. Baby Noah lies on a blanket on the floor. Ariel has her head down low, and the baby is trying to grab tufts of her hair. He's probably never seen such a bright color on a human head before.

I sit on the floor to the side and watch. Noah came home from the hospital a few days ago, but this is the first time I have seen him.

Nicki looks at me, trying to see what I think. "M, this is Noah. I mean, obviously." She laughs nervously.

I stare down at the baby. He has thick black hair that sticks straight up. His eyes are too far apart, but there is something pure looking about him. Something that is like goodness. He has bruises and bandages on his arms and a thick swatch of gauze and tape across his chest and down the side. He wears only a diaper. It has little Elmos dancing around the top. His tiny legs look very brown next to its perfect whiteness.

"Nick, he is adorable!" I reach out a finger and ruffle that funny hair. He freezes for a second, hand mid-reach, and then continues his efforts to touch Ariel's hair. It's too short for him to really grab.

"Ariel, you guys have the same hair, only different colors!" I snicker.

She laughs. "I guess we do." She turns back to Noah and says in a voice I have never heard before (the kind of voice people use on babies to be cute, but that actually sounds stupid), "Does wittle Noah-boa's hair wook wike Auntie Ariel's?"

Noah blows spit bubbles and pedals his legs in response, even though he probably can't hear her.

Nicki floats over to her desk and straightens the pencil holder by a millimeter. "My mom and dad went to a movie. I'm babysitting. This is the first time they have gone out alone, I mean without him, in a really long time."

I continue to watch Noah and Ariel as I say, "So he's pretty much okay now?"

Nicki begins sorting her paper clips into color groups. "Not really *okay* okay, but the doctors say he's stable for now. He needs to get stronger for a few months, and then they'll try another surgery to fix his heart."

Nicki finds a knot of paper clips and is working to free each one and put it in its color group. She must have aced kindergarten.

I go on, curious about Noah. "So, um, besides the heart thing, will he get better . . . ?" I mean about being retarded, but I can't say it. Obviously I know Down syndrome doesn't just go away, but I don't know if it's treatable or improvable or whatever.

Nicki expertly frees a red clip. "You can say 'challenged,' 'special,' 'different,' or 'retarded,' Mattie. Though no one really says retarded anymore, but technically that's what he is. Anyway, we won't really know how severe it is until he grows more, gets older."

I nod. It's so sad, but he is so cute. I don't know how I'd feel if I had a baby brother like this.

Ariel chimes in, "He seems very cool to me." She rubs her head carefully on his upper arm, where there are no bruises or bandages, and he giggles. She's right, he's an excellent baby.

"Yeah, he already has a personality. He's a goofball, but very stubborn," Nicki tells us. "I can't believe I wanted him to be . . . gone." She is speaking very softly, as if Noah might hear and be offended.

I look Nicki hard in the eye. "You didn't really, Nick, it was just a hard time. And I think we all wished for the wrong stuff, somehow."

"Thank god that magic wasn't real. I mean, what if that ritual, that poem of change, really did change things just like we wanted?"

I cross my arms, stare at the carpet. "Well, I still think the book is true and real magic. Look at everything that has changed and happened!"

Ariel rocks back on her heels and makes a peace sign with her fingers. "Guys, guys, let's not debate the magic thing anymore, okay?"

Nicki and I both nod. I don't want to ruin the day, and I know we just disagree about this, and we're not going to change our minds. Ariel is siding with Nicki too, saying it was all a bit silly.

I feel like they have abandoned something important by dismissing the book like this. Maybe they can because they are starting to deal with their problems, but I still look at the book almost every night, running my fingers over the bumpy purple cover and thumbing through the thick pages. Honestly, I don't think my mom can get better without the power of the undoing ritual. I could end up with my dad if she doesn't. So I still memorize rituals and practice chanting. I know there's something to it. It makes me feel sort of lonely somehow, even here with Nicki and Ariel, to be the only one to still honor our book and its power. But anyway.

"We should take Noah out!" Ariel says suddenly, eyes snapping to Nicki. "Can we?"

Nicki is still neatly putting her colored clips in tidy piles within the tray. She considers. "You mean, for a walk or something?"

"Yeah, just down Park or whatever. I bet he'd love it!"

Noah babbles something that sounds like "dwa," as if he's agreeing with Ariel.

Nicki considers. "I think it would be okay. But I should call my parents first and make sure."

She calls, and it's fine. We get out the stroller from the hall closet and load the basket thing underneath with diapers, wipes, blankets, bottles of formula and water, extra clothes, a few rattling toys, and a stuffed penguin. We'll only be gone an hour or so, but we want to be prepared.

I hold the baby for the first time just before we put him in the stroller. He feels so solid and warm. He's actually the first baby I have ever held. I didn't expect it ... him ... to be so nice feeling. Then he spits up on my shoulder. It's warm and disgusting as it soaks through my shirt. Nicki and Ariel crack up.

I laugh too, but truthfully, it is making me feel

nauseous, the ripe, gluey smell of formula vomit. "Let's swing by my house so I can change my shirt."

"You can borrow something," Nicki says.

"Your stuff is too tight on me. My house is on the way, and I'll just run in and be fast."

And so we start off, taking turns pushing the stroller. We point out puffy clouds, birds, delivery trucks, and California poppies to Noah. His eyes are wide and interested as we talk.

When we get to my house, Ariel and Nicki wait on the sidewalk and I dash through the door. I don't want to see my mom right now. She might want to finish our fight.

I can't avoid her though. She's sitting in the middle of the floor. She has the heavy kitchen scissors in one hand and a Trader Joe's paper bag is on her other side. I watch as she picks up a CD from a stack and starts cutting. The thing doesn't really cut well, but it cracks and snaps into several shiny, jagged pieces. She tidily puts the fragments in the paper bag.

"What are you doing, Mom?"

"No more computer games, M. It won't bring back your pigs, but maybe it'll help bring *us* back, you know?"

I stare, dumbfounded. Is she insane? Or is this the sanest thing she's done in a long time? Is the spell we cast so long ago finally taking hold? Even without the undoing? I am stunned.

I just raise my eyebrows at her and step around the

pile. "Mom, well, okay then. Whatever. I just need to change my shirt, my friends are waiting outside."

She glances quickly toward the door. "Oh, I see. Well, could you maybe just tell them you're going to stay home now? We have to talk." She snaps the case of Mall Tycoon in half and neatly shreds the paper insert. All the ruined parts go in the bag.

"Later, Mom. Hey, couldn't you just sell those on eBay?"

"Yes, but I'm not."

Well that's pretty darn obvious. "Right now I am going for a walk with my friends."

She nods, shrugs a little. "But come home as soon as you can, okay? We need to clear up a lot, Matilda."

"Sure." I walk quickly to my room, grab a shirt off the floor, throw it on, and rejoin Ariel and Nicki in about one minute. I see Mom struggling to snap a blue CD with the scissors as the door closes. Can I just say . . . *what the hell?* Sorry, but seeing one's mother sitting on the floor calmly destroying computer games calls for some strong language.

Noah is fussing a little. I stare at him, trying to block out the mental image of my mother.

Nicki asks, "Everything all right, Mattie?"

I nod. "Yeah, sure, of course. Let's go!" I could tell them about Mom, the destruction happening as we speak, but I don't want to. I don't even want to think about it.

It All Comes Back to Books and Pigs

We decide to treat ourselves at Loard's Ice Cream. We barely have enough money to get two scoops each, but Nicki finds three quarters in the bottom of the diaper bag, thankfully.

We try to sit and eat our cones, but Noah starts crying and he won't take a bottle or be soothed by any of us. He wants motion, you can tell. He's rocking his small body impatiently, and I know if he could talk he'd tell us to get rolling.

So we walk back down Park Street, on the other side. It's hard to push the stroller and eat an ice-cream cone at the same time, but we are switching off and managing. Noah is happy and quiet again. At crosswalks people talk to him. The vibrations of loud buses and cars startle him and make him jerk and arch his back.

The bookstore is having a sidewalk sale again. A

huge table partially blocks the sidewalk, and we are forced to take Noah out of the stroller to safely get around it. I maneuver the empty stroller around the table with one hand, trying not to drop my dripping cone. Nicki is holding Noah ahead of me, and Ariel is holding both her own cone and Nicki's. Their backs are to me. Which is when I see it.

The purple is unmistakable. It is worn and rough textured, as though old and well used. The barely legible, scrolling, metallic title looks rubbed away. It is worn away in a pattern I know exactly. *This is THE book.* But how can it be? It is devastatingly identical.

Nicki and Ariel are waiting for me up the sidewalk, looking in a store window. I have made it partially around the book table that fills the walkway, and awkwardly I straddle the curb while bracing the stroller. Mocha almond fudge ice cream drips down my wrist. I am frozen like this, awkward, uncomfortable, stunned, as I stare at the book. There's more than one? There's more than one. I guess I always assumed our book was a one-of-a-kind, and to see another instantly sucks the magic right out of it.

"M, come on," Ariel calls to me. Nicki is bouncing Noah on her hip, watching me patiently.

"Yeah, okay, I'm coming." I drop my cone in the gutter and use both hands to hoist the stroller to the other side of the book table.

Ariel scrutinizes me. "You look funny. What's the matter?"

I shrug, give Ariel a blank look. "Nothing, stroller was just caught on the table for a second is all."

"We should head back home I think," Nicki says. "My parents will be home soon."

"And I want to catch the new episode of *Top Chef*"—Ariel taps her blue watch—"It's on in twenty minutes."

"I am going to look in a couple stores real quick, before I go home." I'm not really ready to go home yet. I feel a slick of fear about facing my mom, and I am trying to wrap my head around seeing the other book. "Aunt Winda's birthday is soon, and my mom said I should look around for something. You guys go ahead."

Ariel shrugs. "Okay, Miss M. Call me tomorrow?"

"Yep. Bye!"

I blow Ariel and Nicki a kiss before turning away. I begin walking again, this time alone. At the crosswalk I turn back and watch my friends' retreating backs. From this far away they look like people I don't know. They have such female shapes, I notice, their hips gently rolling as they walk. It gives me a strange feeling seeing them look like this. I feel panicked for a second as I realize my friends are changing.

The pedestrian signal flashes the walking man and I turn back and cross the street. There's a secondhand store I want to go in. It always has an unpredictable assortment of "treasures" in the window.

Today there is one of those scary-looking porcelain dolls with eyes painted into mean shapes, a pair of *Sesame Street* rubber boots, some old-timey jars and blue glass bottles, and a miniature rusting wheelbar-row with a fake plant sitting in it.

I go in. It smells like dust, old paper, dried flowers, and damp towels. It's one of those places that makes you breathe through your mouth. An overweight man behind the counter glances up at me.

There are three rows of floor-to-ceiling shelves in the back of the store. Knickknacks crowd every space. I have never seen so much junk. Who wants to buy baskets with holes, handkerchiefs with someone else's name, ashtrays from Niagara Falls, and all that kind of random stuff? I am wondering at it all when I see the pig.

It is carved out of a silky, light green stone. When I pick it up it is heavy and cool and perfectly smooth against my skin. The pig sits and gazes to the right and slightly up. His nostrils flare delicately as though he is smell-sampling the wind. He looks peaceful. His body is not carved in great detail, but rather it is soft and undefined. If it's possible for a pig to look serene and stirring, this one does. I must have him. There's a price on the bottom: five dollars.

I spent all my money on ice cream. I take the pig to the front of the store. The man looks up from his book. I think I recognize him from Mrs. Rosencrantz's funeral. I remember he paused a long time at the casket.

Alameda is weirdly small—you're always seeing peo-ple that you somehow know. Or maybe that's just how it is for everyone; we keep crossing paths with people who have connections to us. I mean Mrs. Rosencrantz wasn't even my neighbor, but she ended up connecting me to James (not in a good way, but that's old news) and now this guy.

"Um, hi." I smile nervously. "I really want to buy this pig, but I don't have any money right now. I mean I have money at home. Can I come back later? Will you keep it behind the counter for me?"

The man reaches out his hand and takes the pig gently. "Sure I will. I can hold it for two days." I can tell he recognizes me too, but he doesn't say anything.

"I'll be back later on tonight."

"We close at nine o'clock."

I watch him put the pig on a shelf behind him next to a lamp with ugly fake jewels glued all over it.

"Okay, thanks." I turn to go and then think of something and turn back. "Oh, do you buy stuff too?"

The man nods slowly. He has the kind of glasses people have to look over the tops of to see. "We do, but I have to see the items to decide if I want to buy them."

I think of the jumble of junk collecting dust at the back of his store. I purse my lips a little to avoid smirking.

I walk back home quickly. I take those kind of steps that are just a little too long for your legs but that make you feel like you're walking really fast. I wonder if someone saw me from far away if I would look like I am becoming a woman too. I think I am, just kind of slowly.

Discovering Pig Magic

Mom is in the kitchen when I get home. I can tell she has been waiting for me. Her shoulders slump and her eyes are red and turned down at the corners when she looks up.

"Hey, Mom."

"Hi, honey. Did you have a nice time with Ariel and Nicki?"

There isn't time for us to ease into things here, the store closes so soon.

"Will you come with me to a store on Park Street?"

She knits her eyebrows, confused. "M . . . what?"

I take a deep breath and give her what I hope is a firm, serious look. "I need you to put on clothes and walk to Park Street with me."

She breaks eye contact, looks down.

"Mom, please." I don't even know why, but it seems

so important to me right now that she come. I feel like something will break that can never be fixed if she says no.

Her voice is barely more than a whisper. "Yes, okay, Matilda. Okay. I will. We can leave in a few minutes."

She heads to her room, and I head to mine. Two minutes later we are on the sidewalk. She wears jeans and a blue and gold Cal sweatshirt. Her hair is brushed back in a simple ponytail. She looks slightly scared.

We walk without saying much. I swing the heavy bag I carry back and forth in a slow arc. Mom takes my other arm, looping her hand around my elbow. I can feel a slight trembling in her. I feel like I am making her strong right now. It's nice.

At the store the man looks like he hasn't changed positions since I left him. He looks up and smiles. "I guess you weren't lying when you said you'd be right back." He reaches behind him and places the pig on the counter.

Mom approaches slowly, her eyes glued to the pig. "This is why we came here, M?" She picks up the pig and rubs her thumb over the smooth curve of his belly.

I shrug. "Yeah, Mom, it is."

She nods slowly, studying the little figure. Finally she looks up, a big smile spreading across her face. "I didn't bring my wallet though."

"I brought my own money from home." I take the pig from her and carefully place it back on the counter. "Um, could you go over there?" I gesture to a side alcove that is away from the register. I grab the bag I brought and thunk it onto the counter. "I need to do something else."

Mom glances at the bag and then looks at my face. There is a long pause. Finally, she gives my forearm a little squeeze and walks away.

The store guy has been watching with interest, I can tell. He looks at me with a questioning expression. I dump the bag upside down. The book slithers out.

"Will you trade me the pig for this book?" I ask the man.

He takes the oversized purple book in his hands. "I don't generally buy books . . ."

I interrupt him. "This isn't like a reading book . . . it's more like something to collect. Maybe display. It's unique . . ." (Okay, maybe that is a stretch).

He thumbs through it. The fan of pages makes the musty, dusty air swirl for a second.

He looks back up at me and winks. "Sure, why not? One pig for one book of magic."

"You could tell it says magic?" It took us weeks to figure out each of the curling letters, so I am amazed he has read it just like that.

"Oh, does it *say* magic somewhere?" He turns the book over and squints hard at the back cover. "Don't see the word, just thought it looked like a magic book." He doesn't seem to be messing with me; his voice is serious and natural.

I shrug. "Well anyway, thanks."

He wraps my pig up in a piece of newspaper, carefully packing its face in extra crumples. He says, very softly, "This pig has something magical about him too, don't you think?"

"Yeah." It is one of those exactly right moments somehow. I know I'll always remember every detail when I look at my new pig. I take the bag from the man and turn around to look for mom. She is leafing through a box of posters, allowing me to conduct my business privately.

I call to her, "Mom, let's go!"

She comes back over. She has a slight sheen on her forehead, like she has a fever or something.

"Mom? You okay?"

She takes a breath. It sounds like a series of little shudders. Then she laughs a little.

"Well, Miss M, not really, but I think I'm gonna be. You know?"

I nod. I know exactly what she means.

She loops her hand around my arm and we walk out into the night.

Epilogue

I finally got Mom and Dad to agree that El Sombrero's food is nasty, and that we only went there when we were a family because it was habit. I couldn't go on eating the plastic cheese, and my Dad confessed that the meat in the burritos tasted like dog. So now we are sitting in Linguini Pete's, eating piles of pasta. It's delicious. Maybe we should come back here next month too, when Dad comes for his monthly dinner with us. We had all agreed to try new restaurants each time, but man, this alfredo sauce is seriously yummy. I'll have to tell Ariel.

Dad wanted to eat at the sushi bar, but I finally confessed to my secret loathing of sushi, so we agreed on Italian for tonight. Now that he's showing up every month, I bet eventually we'll try every restaurant in Alameda.

Mom looks good tonight. This is the third time this week she's been out. Two days ago we shopped for back-to-school clothes at Mervyns, and yesterday she went by herself and got a manicure. The last six months of therapy have been hard for her. She still feels panicked about going out, but she's doing it. And a little more all the time.

We finish dinner and we are all stuffed and groaning. It is one of those rare, almost hot evenings with a perfectly clear sky. We agree a walk is just the thing we need. We stroll down Park and cut through the mall to the bay path. I use the opportunity to lobby for sailing lessons. Ariel's parents have already agreed, and Nicki's Mom said yes if me and Ariel get to take the lessons. I figure my parents will have to agree finally, considering Nicki's fate will be decided by them as well.

Mom finally says I can do the sailing for sure, and Dad's about to cave in, when our pace slows. The conversation stops and the mood becomes serious. We are all the way over the bridge and onto Bay Farm Island when my mom starts to really panic. Her whole body starts to hum with nerves. She cracks her knuckles. She wants to go back.

"Mom, please, let's just go up the path. Look at this evening. It's gorgeous! I want you to keep walking with us, Mom, you can do this." I realize I am kind of parenting her here, even nagging a teeny bit with my tone, but I suddenly have this spectacular idea.

Dad pats my mom's shoulder uncertainly. "Matilda, if your mom isn't ready to go this far, let's not force it."

I cut him off. "There's something up farther I need her help with though,"—both my parents are looking at me as if I am the mental one—"okay?"

Mom nods. She crosses her arms tightly, her fists balled in her armpits, and starts back up the trail. Dad and I follow her single file.

We've been walking almost ten minutes when I see it. I can't believe I ever missed it before; it is so recognizable, so obvious now. The shape of the tree trunk twists into a shape that's like a wavy heart, and the branches look like fingers pointing straight across to Coit Tower.

I stop and call out to my parents, who turn around and approach me curiously.

"Miss M? What?" Mom cocks her head at me. Dad waits quietly.

"Can you help me dig a hole here?"

"A hole?" Dad furrows his eyebrows in puzzlement. "Why?"

Mom says nothing, just kneels beside me and starts scooping mucky chunks out of the earth where I am kneeling, already digging too. I feel like she knows, but she can't really. A strange, buzzing energy surrounds us as we dig. My dad sits awkwardly on the water side of the trail, ripping grass with his fingers and staring out at the brown pelicans who are fishing nearby. We are all silent. I know the magic of the book is here right now, with me, with us.

My mom is suddenly scratching impatiently in her side of our hole, using both hands to scrape. And like magic, the little pig is in her hand. She clutches him in her palm, awkwardly pushes herself off the ground with the other hand, and walks to the water's edge. She washes him carefully. His ceramic body changes from a dull, muddied grayish color to shiny pink. His gold accents wink merrily in the setting sun.

She hands him to me and I carefully accept him back, cradling him in my pocket. The three of us are squinting into the fading light as we turn back to the trail and head home.

Julie Crabtree received her B.A. in English from the University of California at Davis in 1992 and earned her paralegal certificate in 1994. She worked as a legal administrator until 1999, and then became a freelance writer. Ms. Crabtree has published writing in the *San Francisco Chronicle Magazine, Highlights for Children, MotherVerse,* and *Green Prints.* Passionate about yoga, cooking, and gardening, Julie lives in Crescent City, California, with her husband and two young daughters. *Discovering Pig Magic* is her first novel. Visit the author's Web site at: www.julie-crabtree.com

More Children's Books from Milkweed Editions

If you enjoyed this book, you'll also want to read these other Milkweed novels.

To order books or for more information, contact Milkweed at (800) 520-6455 or visit our Web site (www.milkweed.org).

Perfect
Natasha Friend

The Year of the Sawdust Man
A. Lafaye

The Linden Tree
Ellie Mathews

Remember as You Pass Me By
L. King Pérez

The Summer of the Pike
Jutta Richter

Slant
Laura E. Williams

Milkweed Editions

Founded in 1979, Milkweed Editions is one of the largest independent, nonprofit literary publishers in the United States. Milkweed publishes with the intention of making a humane impact on society, in the belief that good writing can transform the human heart and spirit.

Join Us

Milkweed depends on the generosity of foundations and individuals like you, in addition to the sales of its books. In an increasingly consolidated and bottom-line-driven publishing world, your support allows us to select and publish books on the basis of their literary quality and the depth of their message. Please visit our Web site (www.milkweed.org) or contact us at (800) 520-6455 to learn more about our donor program.

Milkweed Editions, a nonprofit publisher, gratefully acknowledges sustaining support from Anonymous; Emilie and Henry Buchwald; the Bush Foundation; the Patrick and Aimee Butler Family Foundation; the Dougherty Family Foundation; the Ecolab Foundation; the General Mills Foundation; the Claire Giannini Fund; John and Joanne Gordon; William and Jeanne Grandy; the Jerome Foundation; the Lerner Foundation; the McKnight Foundation; Mid-Continent Engineering; a grant from the Minnesota State Arts Board, through an appropriation by the Minnesota State Legislature, a grant from the National Endowment for the Arts, and private funders; Kelly Morrison and John Willoughby; an award from the National Endowment for the Arts, which believes that a great nation deserves great art; the Navarre Corporation; the Starbucks Foundation; the St. Paul Travelers Foundation; Ellen and Sheldon Sturgis; the James R. Thorpe Foundation; the Toro Foundation; Moira and John Turner; United Parcel Service; U. S. Trust Company; Joanne and Phil Von Blon; Kathleen and Bill Wanner; Serene and Christopher Warren; and the W. M. Foundation.

Interior design by Dorie McClelland
Typeset in Warnock Pro
by Dorie McClelland
Printed on acid-free, recycled (100 percent
postconsumer waste) paper
by Friesens Corporation